Something Old,
Something New

Cedar River Daydreams

#1 / New Girl in Town
#2 / Trouble with a Capital "T"
#3 / Jennifer's Secret
#4 / Journey to Nowhere
#5 / Broken Promises
#6 / The Intruder
#7 / Silent Tears No More
#8 / Fill My Empty Heart
#9 / Yesterday's Dream
#10 / Tomorrow's Promise
#11 / Something Old, Something New
#12 / Vanishing Star

Other Books by Judy Baer

Paige
Adrienne

Something Old, Something New

Judy Baer

BETHANY HOUSE PUBLISHERS
MINNEAPOLIS, MINNESOTA 55438

Something Old, Something New
Judy Baer

All scripture quotations not marked otherwise in this publication are from the Holy Bible, New International Version. Copyright © 1973, 1978, International Bible Society. Used by permission of Zondervan Bible Publishers.

Library of Congress Catalog Card Number 90-56210

ISBN 1–55661–183-8

Published by Bethany House Publishers
A Ministry of Bethany Fellowship, Inc.
6820 Auto Club Road, Minneapolis, Minnesota 55438

Printed in the United States of America

In the beginning God created the heavens and the earth.

GENESIS 1:1

The earth is the Lord's and everything in it, the world, and all who live in it.

PSALMS 24:1

Humankind has not woven the web of life. We are but the thread of it. Whatever we do to the web, we do to ourselves. All things are bound together. All things connect. Whatever befalls the earth, befalls also the children of the children.

CHIEF SEATTLE
Address to President Franklin Pierce, 1855

JUDY BAER received a B.A. in English and Education from Concordia College in Moorhead, Minnesota. She has had over seventeen novels published and is a member of the National Romance Writers of America, the Society of Children's Book Writers and the National Federation of Press Women.

Two of her novels, *Adrienne* and *Paige*, have been prizewinning bestsellers in the Bethany House SPRINGFLOWER SERIES (for girls 12–15). Both books have been awarded first place for juvenile fiction in the National Federation of Press Women's communications contest.

Chapter One

"Don't throw that soda can away!" Egg Mc-Naughton's voice crackled anxiously. He lunged for the pop can that Jennifer Golden was about to toss into the large metal garbage can in the hallway of the Cedar River High School.

The last day of school before summer vacation had just ended. Students were pouring out of the doorway in a wide, human river. Lexi Leighton, Egg, Jennifer, Binky McNaughton and Todd Winston were carried along by the big wave. No one had time to comment on Egg's odd behavior as he grabbed the aluminum can from Jennifer's grasp and clutched it to his chest. The hallway was filled with chatter, squeals and murmurs of "Good-bye. See you in the fall."

Lexi glanced down the quickly emptying corridors. Minda Hannaford and her friends in the Hi-Five Club were having a big conference outside the *Cedar River Review* staff room. They were, no doubt, plotting a summer schedule of mischief and grief. Or, perhaps Minda and the Hi-Fives were planning their pool wardrobes. Minda and her friends were always a step ahead in fashion.

Matt Windsor gave the gang a lopsided grin as they passed. He was cleaning out his locker, methodically dumping everything from its bottom into a large gray garbage can.

"Looks like you aren't saving any souvenirs from this semester," Todd commented.

Anna Marie Arnold walked past them on her way to the school office. Lexi couldn't help staring at the thin girl's retreating figure. Anna Marie had changed more than anyone else Lexi had met during the past year. When they'd first become friends, Anna Marie was chunky. If Anna Marie had been overweight before, she was definitely too thin now. Her skin was pale and translucent-looking and her eyes were tired and drawn. Anna Marie was battling an eating disorder.

Suddenly Binky McNaughton gave an ear-splitting scream. "Ohhhhhh. . . !"

Todd stuck his finger in his ear. "What was *that* all about?"

"Summer is here!" Binky waved her arms excitedly. "We're being sprung from this place. Isn't it wonderful? No homework. No rules. No regulations!" she said dreamily.

"Sounds like it's more fun at your house than it is at mine," Jennifer commented. "My mother comes up with more rules and regulations for me in the summer than she does in the winter."

"Bye kids. See you in the fall," a clear, strong voice called from across the hallway. Mrs. Waverly stood in the doorway to her office. "Have a wonderful vacation." The music teacher gave Egg a strange, meaning-filled look. A creeping blush began at the base of Egg's neck and crawled up to his chin. It spread like licks of fire across his cheeks and his ears.

"Are you blushing, Egg?" Lexi asked bluntly.

"What's *that* all about?" Binky wondered.

"You didn't hear?" Todd asked. "Mrs. Waverly caught Egg digging in her garbage can today. She asked him if he'd become some kind of a spy for the *Cedar River Review,* looking for the low-down on her life."

"Oh, Egg, you *didn't!*" Binky gasped.

Egg turned even more red but refused to explain why he'd been caught pawing through his favorite music teacher's garbage.

"Hey, Lexi," Jennifer said, changing the subject. "Have you made your plans for the summer? Will we be able to spend some time together?"

"I hope so. I'm going to work for my father part-time at his veterinary clinic. He has a list of chores for me. And Ben will expect some attention. Other than that . . ."

"You'd better fit me into your schedule," Jennifer said with a shake of her finger. "How about you, Todd?"

"I'm going to work for my brother Mike at his garage. Mike says I have to punch a time clock this year. He's going to be a tough boss. I don't know if I'm looking forward to it or not. At least Mike promised to help me reupholster the seats in my '49 Ford Coupe. That poor old car needs some attention."

Lexi gave Todd an affectionate glance. She'd recently come through a painful time in her life. Her grandfather had died and her grandmother had been diagnosed with Alzheimer's disease. Lexi hadn't handled it well and had driven Todd away for a while. She'd almost lost the best friend she'd ever had. She and Todd were just learning to know each other again. Lexi was grateful for this "starting over" period for her and Todd. She wouldn't make the same mistake twice.

"Frankly, you guys don't sound like any fun at all," Jennifer said in her usual blunt manner. "I'm going to lie around all day and be lazy. I'll sleep late, swim at the pool, paint my toenails . . ."

Lexi grinned at her friend, but didn't say a word. She knew that Jennifer was going to take a summer school class. Jennifer had dyslexia. School was a real struggle for her. Summer school would enable her to take fewer credits during the year. It was just like Jennifer to act like a clown when she was really very bright and conscientious.

"I don't know what I'm going to do this summer." Binky chewed worriedly at her lower lip. "I should do something, shouldn't I? I won't have a baby-sitting job because the little girl I've watched is going to visit her grandparents. I suppose that means I'm going to be broke all summer."

"Jerry's going to be working at the Hamburger Shack full-time. He told me so himself," Jennifer announced.

That news didn't surprise Lexi. Jerry Randall was a rather lonely boy who lived with his aunt and uncle while his parents worked in the Persian Gulf.

"Does anyone know what Anna Marie Arnold will be doing? I haven't had a chance to talk to her."

"Anna Marie called the other night," Lexi said softly. "She told me she'll be traveling with her family. They're going to visit some national parks and stay with relatives along the way."

"I wonder what all the relatives are going to say about Anna Marie's new look." Jennifer referred to the gaunt, anoretic figure that Anna Marie had become in the past months.

Lexi knew that Anna Marie was attending therapy sessions. She prayed nightly for her friend.

"What's Minda up to?" Jennifer's blue gaze fixed on the group of Hi-Fivers huddled together. "No good, I imagine."

Binky, who'd overheard Jennifer's tight-lipped question, answered. "Minda told me she wasn't planning to do anything this summer except sunbathe." Her expression turned wistful. "It must be nice to have enough money in your family so you don't have to worry about finances." She sighed. "I wish I had a job."

Jennifer ignored Binky's complaint. "Sunbathing. I can picture Minda coming back to school in the fall fried to a crispy brown, tossing her golden hair around, and thinking she's really great. Doesn't she know that it's not healthy? Doesn't she know that pale is beautiful?"

Egg made a gurgling sound. "A few minutes ago you said *you* were going to lie around and be lazy, Jennifer. What makes it all right when you do it and bad when Minda does it?"

"You're never going to get over that crush you have on her, are you, Egg?" Jennifer said frankly.

A blush seeped across Egg's features. "And you're never going to get over disliking Minda, are you?"

"I like people who like me. I'll be Minda's friend

when she's willing to be mine."

Before Jennifer could say any more, Matt Windsor sauntered up. "My locker is empty. I'm a free man," he announced. "Now I can get on my motorcycle and ride."

"Going anywhere special?" Egg asked curiously.

"Didn't you hear? I've got a job at Yellowstone National Park for the summer."

"Oooh," Binky gasped. "What are you going to be doing?"

"I'll probably be on a maintenance crew. If I'm lucky, I'll get to work at the big lodge or in one of the gift shops. I'll find out when I get there." Matt glanced at his watch. "I guess I'd better get going. I only have two days before I have to leave. I have lots of packing to do."

"Have a great summer, Matt!" Lexi said with a smile.

"Yeah, the best," Todd clapped his arm around Matt's shoulder.

"Don't forget to send us a postcard," Binky and Egg chimed.

Jennifer gave Matt a lazy smile. "Be sure to say good-bye before you leave."

Matt grinned and tweaked her cheek as they walked through the school's outer doors. "I might even write you a letter, Jennifer."

The group watched Matt swing his leg across the seat of his motorcycle. Binky looked very sad as she watched Matt ride away.

"Bink? Are you okay?" Lexi asked as they walked across the parking lot toward Todd's blue Ford Coupe.

"I was just thinking about Matt leaving for the summer."

"Why are you so blue?" Jennifer chimed. "*I'm* the one who'll miss Matt."

"I know that," Binky said with a crooked smile, "but his leaving reminded me that Harry will be going too."

"I'm sorry, Binky," Jennifer apologized. "I forgot. Me and my big mouth."

Harry Cramer's friendship had done more for Binky's self-esteem than anyone could have imagined. But now that Harry had graduated, things would change for them.

"Harry's going to summer school at the University of Minnesota. I was worried about having to say good-bye to him in the fall and now he's leaving early." Binky spread her hands hopelessly.

"He'll be coming home to visit, won't he?" Jennifer asked.

"I don't know. He's taking a heavy load. His parents are encouraging him to get involved with things on campus. They've told him it's not smart to be tied down to a girl back home." Binky's pale eyes flickered. "It made me angry at first. But the more I think about it, I guess they're right. I don't want to ruin his time at college because I'm waiting for him here at home."

"That's pretty grown up of you, I'd say," Jennifer blurted. "I'd be furious."

"We're still friends. Besides, I'm too young for a steady boyfriend."

"How sensible can you get?" Jennifer stared at Binky.

Binky's eyes began to twinkle. "Maybe I'll work really hard and get my grades up. That way, I can earn a scholarship and go to the University myself. We'll be together again sooner than you think."

"There's always the post office and stamps, right Binky?" Lexi said slyly. "And the telephone. Long-distance calls."

"I know." Binky groaned. "Harry and I promised to write or call each other every day. Where am I going to get the money for that?"

"Here we go again," Jennifer said with a moan. "Binky's penniless and without a boyfriend. What are we going to do?" It was difficult to take anything too seriously when Jennifer was around. She was so blunt, outspoken and ready to speak her mind that she didn't give people a chance to feel sorry for themselves.

Binky snapped her fingers. "Speaking of writing letters, has anyone heard from Peggy Madison?"

"Peggy should be coming home in a few weeks," Lexi murmured. "I got a letter from her yesterday."

Only Lexi and Todd knew that Peggy had become pregnant by Chad Allen. She'd left school to stay with her physician uncle in Arizona, to complete her pregnancy and give the baby up for adoption. Lexi had suffered through much of the heartbreak with Peggy. Soon Peggy would come back to Cedar River to make a fresh start with her life.

"I've really missed Peggy," Binky said. "Haven't you?"

Silently, Lexi wondered what it would be like to see Peggy again. Would she have changed? How could she have given birth to a child and *not* be changed? Lexi knew that the girl who returned would not be the same as the old Peggy Madison, the first friend Lexi had made when she came to Cedar River.

A touch of apprehension skittered through Lexi. What would Peggy be like? Would they still be friends?

Chapter Two

Ben squatted by a newly planted tree in the Leighton yard. It was little more than a twig sticking out of the ground. His chubby, dimpled knees were bent and his curious nose was only inches from the two little green leaves that sprouted from the top of the sapling. Ben's trike lay on its side nearby.

"Did you fall over, Ben?" Lexi asked.

"I crashed." Ben made a roaring sound in his throat. "Boom!"

"Are you hurt?"

Ben didn't answer. He peered more closely at the baby tree. "Where do trees go when they die, Lexi?"

"They get turned into houses or paper, or logs for someone's fireplace."

"So they don't die. Not really. They just go somewhere else and be something else."

"You could say that." Lexi watched her little brother cautiously. She could sense he was in one of his question-asking moods. One never knew what might come out of Ben at times like these.

"It's like going to heaven, then, isn't it? We don't die. We go somewhere else and be something else." He smiled sweetly at his sister. "Right?"

Ben never failed to amaze Lexi. He flung himself backward on the lawn and stared at the sky. "What makes the sky blue?" He kicked his feet in the air and rolled from side to side. A robin flew overhead. "Can birds think?"

Suddenly Ben flipped to his belly and stared between the blades of grass. "What's dirt made of?" He squinted deeply, watching something in the grass. "How do spiders walk with so many legs? Why don't they trip?" Ben scrambled to his hands and feet and pretended to walk like a spider. He fell nose first into the grass. When he rolled over, he squinted accusingly at Lexi. "You aren't answering my questions."

"Then ask me something I *can* answer, buddy. I don't know why spiders don't get their legs tangled!"

"When is Peggy coming home? Will she be happy to see us?"

Suddenly Lexi wished she *did* know if birds could think. It was a far simpler question to answer.

As the days had gone by, Lexi had grown more and more apprehensive about meeting Peggy again. Binky, on the other hand, was excited at the prospect of seeing her old friend.

"When Peggy gets back, I think we should have a party," Binky announced as she served a volleyball over the net in the Leighton's yard. "Summer's a great time for parties, don't you think? It would be a nice 'welcome home' for her. We could invite Peggy's friends from the basketball team. They're hoping she'll play with them again next year. We could have it at your house, Lexi. Your mom is great about letting you have friends over. We could make pizza. Peggy *loves* homemade pizza!" She was so busy talking that she ignored the ball that Todd returned, allowing it to drop at her feet.

"We win!" Todd yelled. "That's four games to zero. "You've got to start paying attention, Binky."

"It's not my fault we lose. Egg stands in place and swings his arms like he's a windmill. We can't win like that."

"Your mouth is what runs like a windmill!" Egg retorted. "Flap, flap, flap. You must talk a million words a minute. You should get a job as a disc jockey, Binky. You could talk all you wanted—and for once I could turn you off."

Todd skillfully interrupted to ask Egg, "What about you, Egg? What are you going to do this summer? You didn't tell us the other day." The question sidetracked Binky. She looked expectantly at her brother.

Egg blushed a shade of pink that reminded Lexi of a strawberry ice cream sundae. "Me?" his voice crackled self-consciously.

"Of course, you," Todd said impatiently. "What are your plans for the summer?"

"Well . . . I . . . uh . . ."

"Don't you know?" Todd insisted.

"Sort of," Egg admitted.

"So, spill the beans, Egg! How are you going to earn your spending money?"

"Crushing cans."

Everyone, including his own sister, stared at him blankly. "What?"

Lexi cleared her throat. "If you'll excuse me a minute, I'll get us some lemonade." She vanished into the kitchen.

"Crushing cans." Egg's ears turned red.

"This is the first *I've* heard about it," Binky said. "When did you decide this?"

"I just figured it out a few nights ago," Egg admitted. "I was going to mow lawns, but I started reading about recycling. I decided that that's what I should do."

"Recycling what?" Binky asked suspiciously.

"Aluminum cans." Egg stared at his sister as if the space between her ears were empty. "Don't look at me that way. It's not a harebrained idea." He smiled a goofy, embarrassed grin at Lexi as she returned with the lemonade and a stack of glasses. "Actually, that's why Mrs. Waverly looked at me so strangely after school today."

"Because you're going to crush cans?"

"No, because she caught me digging in her garbage. I found four pop cans in her trash!"

"So you'll spend the summer looking through garbage?" Binky put her thumb and index finger to her nose and squeezed it tightly. "Phew. I don't want anything to do with you if *that's* your job for the summer."

"Don't laugh," Egg said indignantly. "I can make some big bucks recycling aluminum cans. The people at the recycling center pay for aluminum by the pound. All I have to do is collect what other people throw away and turn it in for money."

"I can see it all now," Binky said sarcastically, "another year of Egg McNaughton's being broke."

"I'm not *just* going to recycle cans," he said. His face grew pink again. "I'm going to open a little business on the side. I worked it out last night. I'll hang signs around town offering to clean out garages and haul away junk. People are always looking for a handyman to do that sort of thing. It might as well be me. If there's anything that can be recycled, I can take it to the recycling center while I'm doing my other job. Isn't that a great idea?"

Lexi could see Egg's enthusiasm growing as he spoke.

"I've been thinking about it since Mom began saving old newspapers and glass jars. She says we're all part of this earth. How we treat it will make a difference in the way it treats us. If we fill it with garbage and junk, it's not going to be beautiful or grow green things for food. The way I see it, if I can make a difference and still earn some money at the same time, I'll have a great summer. Besides, we need to conserve our resources," Egg lectured. "We're wasting things that can't be replaced."

"What am *I* doing to fill the earth with garbage?" Binky asked.

"You throw away sheets of paper that don't have much writing on them," Egg accused.

"Well, yes, but . . ."

"You should use the back of those sheets for other notes. Paper is made from trees. When you waste paper, it's just like killing trees."

"Ooooh," Binky's eyes grew wide. "I never thought about it that way."

"Before you throw anything away, you should ask yourself if it can be recycled or reused." Egg's voice grew squeaky with enthusiasm. "We should buy paper products like napkins, paper towels and toilet paper, only in white. The dyes in the colored paper are pollutants." He pointed a scrawny finger at Binky. "And you always buy fast-food sandwiches that come in styrofoam cartons. You should ask to have them wrapped in paper. That foam stuff doesn't decompose no matter how long it lies around."

"You aren't doing so great yourself," Binky retorted. "You're the guy who lets the water faucet run while you're brushing your teeth. And you use the washing machine for just one pair of dirty jeans. What do you have to say about that?"

"You're right, Binky." Egg looked sheepish. "I guess we all have a lot to learn about waste and about saving our environment."

Just then, Ben walked onto the porch carrying the goldfish bowl Lexi had purchased for him at the pet shop. Water slopped out the sides of the bowl as he held it out for his sister to see. "Lexi, my fish is swimming upside down." The goldfish was floating belly up.

Todd reached for the bowl. "Did you find your fish like this, Ben?" He eyed the sticky flakes of fish food adhering to the sides of the bowl.

"Uh huh. He was okay at lunchtime."

"Did you feed him lunch, Ben?"

"Breakfast too. Fishy was hungry."

Lexi and Todd exchanged knowing glances. "How *much* did you feed him?"

Ben reached into his pocket and pulled out a canister of fish food. It was a quarter empty. "This much."

"Ben, that's enough food to last a fish a month, not a day! Didn't Mom tell you not to feed him again until tomorrow?"

Ben's lip quivered. "But he didn't like the other food. It was icky."

Todd stuck his finger into the small canister. "This is pretty icky too, Ben. Why are these flakes so sticky?"

"I cooked him some food," Ben explained, "like I cook brownies."

Lexi peered into the container. "What did you put in his food, Ben?"

"Sugar, oil, salt . . ." Ben ticked off the ingredients on his fingers. "Just a little bit."

"Oh Ben! Fishy couldn't eat that!"

"You've got an oil spill in your fish bowl!" Egg chortled.

"Be quiet, Egg." Binky jabbed him in the ribs. "You'll make Ben feel bad."

"Is Fishy dead?" Ben inquired.

"I'm afraid so, sweetheart."

"Is he like Grandpa and the trees?"

Lexi laughed softly as the others stared. "Yes he is, Ben. Fishy has gone somewhere else to be something else."

"Fertilizer, in this case," Egg muttered.

"I won't ever cook for my fish again," Ben said solemnly as a huge tear poised on the brink of an eyelash.

"Let's go explain what happened to Mom. Maybe this afternoon we can get you another fish."

"Two fish? I think Fishy was lonely."

As Lexi led her little brother away, her voice floated back to her friends. "Benjamin Leighton, you are a little con-man. *Two* fish?"

When Lexi returned, she was shaking her head.

"At least he took the death of his fish rather well. Fortunately, we'd had a talk about what happens to things when they die. He's handling it better than I am."

"It's everywhere. I told you so." Egg's shoulders drooped glumly. "Oil spills in fishbowls. Gunk in Cedar River. What's next?"

"This conversation reminds me of the film they showed us last month in the gym. Remember?" Jennifer blurted.

"It was scary too." Binky shuddered. "The narrator said that if people didn't start taking care of the planet, terrible things would happen."

"The ozone layer in the earth's atmosphere is being destroyed," Todd said. "That's something we can't restore."

"What happens if we don't have an ozone layer?" Binky asked. Her pixy face furrowed into a worried frown.

"A wider spectrum of light is allowed into the atmosphere," Todd explained. He was the scientist in the group, always getting A's in that class. "One of the results is an increased incidence of skin cancer."

Because people weren't taking care of the planet, even *sunlight* was becoming dangerous! Lexi listened intently as her friends talked about the ways in which human beings had not taken care of the planet God had given them.

Lexi remembered a Bible verse from Psalms she'd heard in church only a week ago. "The earth is the Lord's and everything in it." The earth belonged to the Lord—it was *God's* creation that people were ruining!

"Lexi, is something wrong?" Todd asked.

"I was thinking about one of the Bible verses that Pastor Tom read in church on Sunday. She quoted the passage. "We're ruining God's beautiful earth!"

"But what can *we* do about it? We're just kids."

A look of determination settled on Egg's face. Lexi had seen that expression before. Once Egg decided to do something, there was no stopping him.

"We can help. I know we can," he said. "I'm not sure how, but I'm going to find out!"

Chapter Three

"I've got two cards left. One of them is the *Old Maid*. Which one are you going to choose?" Lexi held her cards beneath her little brother's nose and waved them enticingly.

Ben looked at the game card in his little fist and then at the pair Lexi held. "I don't want to be the *Old Maid*," he said with a pout.

"You have to pick the right card then."

"Eenie, meenie, miney, moe . . ." he moved his finger from one card to the other and back again. "Which one should I pick, Lexi?"

Lexi pointed to a card. "Pick this one."

Ben looked at her suspiciously, "Huh-uh. That's the *Old Maid*."

"All right. Then pick this one." Lexi moved her finger to the other card.

"Huh-uh. That's the *Old Maid*."

"They can't *both* be the *Old Maid*, Ben."

Ben's lip protruded. "You're tricking me, Lexi."

Lexi and Ben went through this every time they played the game. Ben, who had Down's syndrome, loved games. While they played, Mrs. Leighton baked cookies at the counter nearby.

"Cookie, anyone?" Mrs. Leighton pulled a pan of fresh hot chocolate chip cookies from the oven. "These will be cool in just a minute."

"I'll take one," Lexi said.

"I'll take ten," Ben announced.

"I should have made a double batch! Are you sure you wouldn't be happy with just one or two?"

"No, ten is fine." Ben grabbed a card from Lexi's hand. "Oh, no!" He groaned as Lexi plucked the match to her remaining card from his hand.

"I'm the *Old Maid!*"

"I won." Lexi reached to give her brother a hug.

"Boys can't be old maids," Ben pointed out. "Ha, ha. You didn't win at all."

"You can be an Old Bachelor, then," Lexi said cheerfully.

"What's a bachelor?"

"A man who isn't married," Lexi explained.

Ben thought about that for a moment. His face cleared. "Oh, that's all right. I'm not married. I'll be the Old Bachelor."

"Will you two put your game away?" Mrs. Leighton asked. "I need the table to spread out these cookies so they can cool." As Lexi was clearing away the clutter, the telephone rang.

"Lexi. This is Egg." He was agitated. His normally squeaky voice sounded badly in need of oil. "I'm calling a meeting at the Hamburger Shack. Can you be there in fifteen minutes?"

"I suppose so, but I'd like to know—"

"I'll explain then. Good-bye."

"Now what was that all about?" Lexi wondered as she put the receiver down.

Lexi's mother turned to her. "What did you say?"

"That was Egg McNaughton. He's calling a meeting at the Hamburger Shack in fifteen minutes."

"What kind of a meeting?"

Lexi shrugged. "I don't know. He wouldn't tell me."

"Isn't that just like Egg?" Mrs. Leighton chuckled. "He's always so enthusiastic about whatever he's doing."

"Sometimes he's just a little *too* enthusiastic. I suppose I'd better go, though. You never know what Egg will be up to next. Do you mind, Mom?"

"Not at all. I'm a little curious myself. Ben can help me with the cookies, can't you Ben?"

"Cookies," Ben echoed. His face was already smeared with chocolate and his fingers coated with crumbs.

"If you have too much help like Ben, you're not going to have any cookies left," Lexi pointed out.

"Have a good time at the Hamburger Shack, Lexi."

Lexi glanced into the mirror and tossed her thick dark hair. She was wearing one of her own designs— an oversized tie-dyed T-shirt and leggings to match.

Lexi liked sewing and fashioning her own clothing. Many times she'd had to stand alone for what she believed. So she never felt compelled to follow fashion trends. She preferred to make her own.

Lexi half-walked, half-jogged toward the Hamburger Shack. She met Jennifer heading in the same direction.

"Going to the meeting?" Jennifer asked.

"What's Egg up to this time?"

"Who knows with him? He actually sounded upset."

"Egg gets upset easily, you know."

"That boy thrives on a cause."

Both of them were reminiscing about the days of the past winter when Egg had thrown himself into weight lifting and health foods. He'd almost gone too far. He'd even considered taking steroids to bulk up his body. That memory caused a worried frown to settle on Lexi's forehead. Egg could come up with some crazy schemes.

Jennifer glanced at Lexi questioningly. "How are things going for you and Todd now that you're back together again?"

"It's different," Lexi admitted. "I think we're more considerate of each other now. We both realize how special our friendship is and that we came very close to ruining it. I never knew how easily a misunderstanding could tear friends apart." Lexi shuddered. "It's frightening, really."

The rest of the gang had already assembled at the Hamburger Shack when the girls arrived. They were sitting in their favorite booth at the back of the restaurant. Egg was at one end of the table, looking stern.

Todd was seated on the bench behind the table. Lexi smiled shyly when his gaze caught hers. He patted the bench and slid over. As she slipped into the spot, he put his arm around her and gave her a gentle squeeze.

Impatiently, Egg pushed an armful of books and newspapers across the table. His face was flushed a bright pink and his Adam's apple bobbed wildly.

Whatever this meeting was about, Lexi mused, it had certainly made Egg excited.

Just then, Jerry Randall came to the table to take their orders. "I'll take a cherry cola," Jennifer told him.

"Me too," chimed Binky.

"Lexi and I will have a banana split," Todd said. "Two spoons, please."

"And I'll have a chocolate malt," Egg said. "Heavy on the chocolate and extra heavy on the malt, please." As Jerry turned to leave, Egg caught the corner of his apron. "Be sure everything's served in glass dishes."

"What other kind of dishes are there?" Jerry frowned.

"That just shows how uneducated you are." Egg glared at him. "Bring everything to us in glass dishes, please. They can be washed and used again."

Jerry walked away shaking his head.

"It's worse than I thought," Egg announced dramatically. "Much, much, *much* worse." He shuffled his long thin fingers through the books, magazines and newspapers spread on the table. "I've been at the public library reading all day. The situation is much more serious than I thought it would be."

"What are you talking about, Egg?" Jennifer asked.

"I spent last night and all of today reading about the environment." Egg looked truly worried. "We're ruining the planet we're living on, absolutely destroying it. There won't be anything left of it for our children or our grandchildren if we keep treating the earth the way we've been treating it in the past few years. Do you realize what that means?"

"Our grandchildren will have to live on Mars?"

Egg glared at his sister so sternly that she almost ducked beneath the table. "This isn't a time for jokes, Binky. I'm scared. Really scared. Take disposable diapers, for example."

Binky giggled. "Why are you worrying about the earth one minute and diapers the next?"

"Do you know how many disposable diapers Americans throw away every year?" He paused dramatically. "Billions."

"Billions?"

"And do you know how many trees it takes to make the paper that goes into those diapers? Millions."

"Millions?" Binky was beginning to sound like an echo.

"Besides that, can you imagine how disposable diapers . . ." Egg made a face, "contaminate the ground?"

"Oh, yuck, Egg," Binky squealed.

"Well, it's true. And diapers are just one example of what we're talking about. Not every family has a baby, but every family does have garbage they throw away every day. If we're not careful, our planet will be overrun with plastic—things that will lie in landfills for five hundred years! Our water will be contaminated gunk!"

Todd and Lexi stared down at the banana split Jerry had brought them. "Suddenly, I don't feel very hungry," Todd commented.

"This conversation doesn't help one's appetite," Lexi agreed.

"Now you know how I've been feeling ever since I started reading these articles. Imagine how I felt when I read this headline over breakfast." Egg waved a newspaper in the air.

"What's that about? More diapers?" Jennifer eyed the newspaper suspiciously.

Dramatically, Egg spread the newspaper out in front of them. Lexi's eyes grew wide as she read the headline across the front page of the Cedar River paper.

IS CEDAR RIVER POLLUTED? SCIENTISTS TO BRING IN VERDICT THIS WEEK.

"Cedar River? Polluted? It can't be." Lexi thought of the beautiful crystal-clear water that meandered through the center of town. Cedar River was one of the prettiest rivers Lexi had ever seen. The town had taken advantage of its beauty by placing parks, golf courses and housing developments on both banks.

Lexi and Ben had taken many walks through the park to the river. They'd stood at the water's edge and watched it ripple and bubble across the smooth, silky-looking sand on the bottom. Ben loved to watch the water because he could see an occasional fish dart past.

"This newspaper article says the mayor is worried about Cedar River. Too many people are throwing garbage into it and contaminating the water. Have you been to the river lately?"

"No." After Lexi's grandmother had been diagnosed with Alzheimer's disease and had come to live with them, all the patterns in Lexi's life had changed.

"Well, it's gross down there." Egg made a face.

"There are soda pop cans and candy wrappers and—"
Suddenly, he pushed away from the table. "Let's go down there now! I want you to see for yourself."

"Awww, Egg! We believe you. Don't make us leave now."

"Yeah, Egg, we understand."

"I don't think you do. Come on." He herded the groaning and complaining group toward the door.

"Let's just see what Egg is talking about," Todd finally suggested. "Then he'll be happy and we won't have to listen to this anymore."

"This had better be good . . . or bad . . . or whatever," Binky muttered. "The boy is slipping off the edge, cracking up, going ga-ga over garbage . . ."

Only Lexi was eager to go. She hadn't been to the park for weeks. She was looking forward to sitting on a bench and watching the water. But the ominous newspaper headline had Lexi worried. Would the park be the same?

Chapter Four

The arched entryway with the words "Welcome to Cedar River Park" looked as if it could use a clean-up job. There was a potato chip bag caught at the base of the sign, and someone had wrapped toilet paper around one of the posts.

"Vandals," Egg muttered, stomping ahead of the group like a hunter stalking his prey. "Pigs."

The rest of the park wasn't much better. Soda pop cans and candy bar wrappers littered the ground. As they neared the river, the trash increased. It was obvious that this was a popular picnic spot by the number of food wrappers and paper napkins strewn about.

"Yuck! Who'd want to spend time down here?" Jennifer wondered, picking her way through the junk.

"Not me." Binky edged her way toward the water. "If I want to spend time in a mess, I can go to my bedroom." She paused at the edge of the bank. "What's this?"

"Lots of trash washed into the river with that rain last night," Egg commented.

"This is disgusting!" Binky shrieked. "What did

I just step in? Aaauuuggghh!" She jumped back and began wiping her feet on the grass. "It squished! And it smells!"

"Relax, Binky," Todd said. "You stepped on a dirty diaper. That rain we had last night really made things a mess."

"I'll have to burn my shoes! I'll never wear them again!"

"When you first started talking, Egg, I thought that worrying about disposable diapers sounded pretty farfetched, but when you see something like that . . ." Jennifer stared at Binky's defiled shoes and looked faint.

It was easy to ignore the idea that somewhere, far away, garbage was filling up holes in the earth. It was not so easy to accept the fact that garbage was floating along the banks of beautiful Cedar River, making it ugly and contaminated. Suddenly, this environmental thing Egg was babbling about had become a reality. Their own Cedar River was in danger!

"It makes me want to cry to think that the river is so junked up," Binky said, her lower lip trembling. "We used to come down here for picnics every Sunday when we were kids."

"Remember how Mom made us pick up all our garbage and put it in the trash cans in the park?" Egg said morosely. "She said that Cedar River was the town's 'best asset' and that we should keep it clean."

"It's true! But now people have picnics and leave their stuff to blow around in the wind." Jennifer looked indignant.

Just then a whimpering sound came from behind a nearby tree.

"What was that?"

"Just the wind, I think."

"It sounded like an animal to me." Todd disappeared into the shrubbery. Seconds later he reappeared, carrying something in his arms.

It was a little white kitten, just a few months old. It was thin and frightened, its eyes popping from its head and a panicky sound coming from its throat. Most horrifying of all was the fact that it was tangled in a web of plastic rings—the kind that hold six-packs of soft drinks together. Each time it moved a leg, the ring around its neck tightened, choking the animal. The kitten struggled to get away from Todd.

He carefully set the kitten on the ground and, pulling a pocket knife from his jean pocket, began to cut away the twisted plastic. Lexi saw the terror in the kitten's eyes.

When the animal was free it struggled to its feet, swaying weakly, uncertain what to do next.

"Go home, kitty. You're okay now." Todd stroked its matted fur, and the kitten darted away.

"You saved its life!" Binky squealed. "That poor little thing would have died if you hadn't come along."

"Probably," Todd agreed somberly. "He would have starved or choked to death."

Jennifer's eyes were wide as saucers. "Who was stupid enough to throw those plastic rings on the ground?"

"Lots of people, by the looks of it," Lexi muttered, kicking at the trash beneath her feet. "This is horrible."

"Now do you see what I've been talking about?"

Egg said fiercely. "Now do you understand why it's so important that we get involved with the environment?"

"You bet!"

"Poor kitty. We should make sure things like that don't happen again."

Lexi, Jennifer and Binky all wore determined expressions. It was Todd who brought them back to reality.

"We've all agreed things are getting pretty gross, a fact we've ignored until Egg brought it up. But the question still is, what can a bunch of kids do?" Todd looked at his friends. "We're not politically powerful. We can't stop people from dumping waste into the river or filling landfills with plastic."

Binky promptly threw her hands in the air and wailed, "It's hopeless. It's hopeless. We're going to live in a pile of muck. I can see it all now."

"It is pretty discouraging, isn't it?" Jennifer said. "I don't even know if I dare tell my cousin to stop using disposable diapers on her baby!"

Binky tucked her tiny pointed chin into her hand and gave a deep sigh. "I'm very depressed," she announced. "I feel so helpless."

Egg tapped a finger on Binky's shoulder. "Don't give up yet, you guys. You just learned about how bad pollution can be. Are you already giving up, saying there's nothing you can do?"

"We *are* just a bunch of kids," Binky pointed out sarcastically. "What's your big idea to change that?"

"I don't want to change the fact that we're kids. But there are things that we can do. First of all, the city's planning to have an emergency clean-up day on the banks of Cedar River. We can all take part in that. We can start making our own plans to save the environment."

"I don't mind helping to clean up Cedar River," Binky said, "but I don't see what I can do about the environment."

"Your problem is that you're thinking too big," Egg said. "We have to start small, with little things."

"What do you mean, 'little things'?"

"We have to start thinking of the earth as our home. Each thing we do around our home should be to help protect it, not hurt it."

"Such as?" Binky was looking skeptical again.

"When we carry our lunches to school next fall, we can reuse the plastic bags our sandwiches are wrapped in. They can be used again the next day. Better yet, we could wrap our sandwiches in waxed paper."

"What good will that do?"

"It'll be one less piece of plastic used. One less piece to be put in a landfill. Besides, it takes a lot of chemicals to make plastic and that's hard on the earth, too."

"I don't see how one little plastic bag . . ."

"If every single person in the whole world reused their plastic bags or their jars or their boxes rather than buying new and throwing the others away, it would begin to make a difference."

"Well, of course, if every person in the world did that . . ." Binky agreed.

"We've got to start somewhere. Why don't we start here in Cedar River? One person threw those plastic rings on the ground. One person—Todd—

saved that kitten by cutting away those rings. One person *can* do a lot!"

"You've got to admit that *for once* he makes sense."

"Thanks, I think," Egg gave Jennifer a sinister glare.

"My dad always cuts up the junk mail and uses the unprinted backs for scrap paper."

"I suppose we could do that instead of buying those cute little colored packs of notepaper at the drugstore."

"Now you're catching on! Don't toss things out without seeing how many other ways they can be used first."

"I realize it's important, Egg," Binky said, "but it still doesn't sound like much."

"There are other things we can do, Binky. You especially."

"What do you mean by that?"

"You could shut off the lights behind you when you leave a room. It wastes a lot of energy to keep a light bulb burning unnecessarily."

"Oh," Binky looked embarrassed. "I do that sometimes, don't I."

"After you wash and dry your hair, you throw the towel in the dryer. If you'd walk outside and hang it on the clothesline, you'd save a lot of energy. And," Egg added, warming to his subject, "you could take short showers instead of your usual prolonged ones, or those bubble baths where you fill the bathtub to the brim and float around like a beached whale."

"Give up my bubble baths?" Binky looked indignant. "Not unless you quit letting the water run when you brush your teeth. You could fill a whole bathtub with all the water that goes down the drain while you're scrubbing your molars."

"It sounds like there are plenty of things that we can do," Todd said. He found a seat on the park bench, brushed it off with his hand and gingerly sat down.

"I'm willing to try," Lexi volunteered as she sat down beside him. "It shouldn't be so hard to recycle things, or turn off the dry cycle on the dishwasher and let the dishes air dry."

"Would that help?" Jennifer wondered.

"Think about it. Every person who isn't wasting something is saving it. It may not seem like we're helping a lot, but it certainly can't hurt. Not everyone can afford to plant new trees, or reclaim landfills, but we can all separate our bottles and cans or save our newspapers and take them to a recycling center. Multiply that by every person and that's quite a lot."

Suddenly Lexi asked, "Do you remember the story in Luke 19? The one about the man who gave his three servants money while he went on a trip?"

"Here it comes," Jennifer said with a chuckle. Lexi's friends accepted the fact that whatever situation they were in, she could find a Bible verse or story that seemed appropriate for the moment.

"The servants were supposed to take care of their master's money. Two of the men invested their money and made more. When the master returned and found his servants had taken such good care of his property, he was very happy."

"So what's the point?" Egg asked impatiently.

"The third servant hadn't done anything with the money his master had given him. He'd simply dug a hole and buried it in the ground. The master had expected his servant to at least bank the money and earn the interest on it, and he became very angry."

"Now, what is *that* supposed to mean?" Egg's family didn't attend church. Sometimes Lexi and her Bible stories amazed him.

"We're just like those servants, Egg. We don't own the earth any more than the servants owned the money that their master gave them. The master gave those men the money expecting them to take care of it and make it earn more. If we ignore what's going on around us, if we just look out for ourselves and take care of the little spot of earth that belongs to us, we're no better than the servant who took his bit of money and buried it in the ground. We don't own the earth any more than the servant owned that money. But, we *are* supposed to take care of it as if it were our very own."

"Makes sense."

Binky peered over at Lexi. "How do you do that?"

"Do what?" Lexi said with a smile, already knowing Binky's next question.

"Always know of a story in the Bible that applies to us. How do you do that?"

"God does it, Binky, not me. He gives us what we need to know in the Bible. It's just up to us to read it and learn what He has to say."

"Sort of like the servants with the money, right?"

"Sort of." Lexi smiled.

"I guess that makes me right, and this project even more important than I thought. If God is on our side, we can't quit now." Egg's face was pink and his Adam's apple bounced like a cork on water. "Everyone has to promise to start taking shorter showers and not let the water run when they brush their teeth."

"And pick up junk on the ground, and *never* leave plastic pop rings or plastic bags lying around."

Egg was so enthused the tips of his ears were turning red. He waved a hand in the air and announced, "And put a brick in every toilet."

"What?" Lexi, Todd, Binky and Jennifer chorused together. "Put a brick *where*?"

Egg flushed a deep red. "Sorry. I got a little carried away. It just says in this material that if you put a displacement device in the toilet tank to reduce the water, it doesn't take so much water to flush. I was just thinking maybe, uh, you know, we could put a brick in every toilet and save a little water?"

"Well, excuse me, but it's going to be a long time before *I* ask anyone to put a brick in their toilet," Binky said. "I think you're slipping over the edge, Egg."

Todd was trying hard not to laugh. "It's not such a bad idea, Binky. It just sounds a little funny. Egg's right. If everyone in Cedar River put a plastic-wrapped brick in their toilet to displace some of the water, think how much water that would save."

Binky did some mental calculations. "Well, I suppose. But it sounds silly to me."

There was no way she could match Egg's enthusiasm, but Lexi knew there was a lot she could do. "Let's get together for the clean-up at Cedar River so we can all work in one spot," she suggested.

"Good idea," Jennifer announced. "We'll put Cedar River back on the map as the prettiest place on earth."

Chapter Five

It had been a long, boring afternoon at the Leighton Veterinary Clinic. Lexi's father was attending a seminar and had left Lexi to answer the phones. She'd made appointments for two poodles, a Siamese cat, three mutts of indeterminate species and a cockatoo. In fact, it was a very uneventful afternoon until Chad Allen arrived.

"Chad!" Lexi didn't mean to sound so surprised to see him, but Chad was rarely around these days. She'd seen him only once since school had recessed for the summer.

"Hi, Lexi. I'm supposed to buy some pet food." He thrust a note at her. "Mom wrote down the brand."

"How many pounds? Five? Ten? Twenty?"

Chad shrugged disinterestedly. "Twenty, I suppose. She didn't say."

Lexi could feel his eyes on her back as she dragged the bag from the pallet where they were stacked. "Here it is. It will only take me a minute to write up the slip." She glanced at him from the corner of her eye. "How are you, Chad?"

He shrugged carelessly. "Okay. Why?"

"Just wondering. What have you been doing this summer?"

"Sleeping."

His answer surprised Lexi. That was the *last* thing she wanted to do on a beautiful summer day!

"Don't you have a job?"

"I work for my dad. He doesn't seem to care. He just puts me on his payroll in the summer. I don't do anything special. Run errands, get gas, mail letters, junk like that."

"That's important."

Chad looked at Lexi doubtfully. "Who are you kidding, Lexi? Any dunce could do it."

She'd never seen Chad this way before. He was often quiet, but never so discouraged or depressed. An odd feeling washed over Lexi. She was sure this mood of Chad's had to do with Peggy's impending return. But did she dare mention Peggy to him now?

"Chad, I . . ."

He looked at her with an alarmed expression. "I . . . I can't talk right now, Lexi. Thanks for the pet food. See ya."

Chad was out the door before Lexi could say anything more. She shivered as she watched him retreat through the glass door. Something in Chad's manner disturbed her. Instinctively she was troubled, but she had no idea why.

———

Mrs. Leighton opened the refrigerator door and stared inside. "I was *sure* I had some eggs in here."

Lexi looked up from the crossword puzzle she was doing at the kitchen table. "Sorry, Mom. Ben and I used the eggs in the brownies we made last night."

"Will you go to the grocery store and pick up a

couple dozen for me, Lexi? We're nearly out of milk too. I'll give you some money. Go to Lyle's Market. It's the closest."

Lexi made a face. "They use plastic grocery bags there."

"They also have paper. Just ask for them." Mrs. Leighton was becoming accustomed to Lexi's enthusiasm for recycling.

"But paper uses up trees."

"Then take the mesh shopping bag in the front closet. I used to do all my shopping with that bag. I'm sorry now that I slipped out of the habit." Mrs. Leighton sat down by her daughter. "Your friend Egg is right. A disposable society isn't good. All the things we throw away have to go somewhere. It's like the old phrase says, 'Out of sight, out of mind.' Once we can't see the trash we've created, we tend to forget about it. But it's still out there, somewhere, having to be moved around, buried, burned or perhaps just piling up, littering God's green earth.

"I can't believe God is happy with the way we've managed the planet. It was in perfect shape when we got it and look at it now." Mrs. Leighton pointed to a magazine article that pictured a trash pit scarring the side of an otherwise beautiful hill.

"Egg would like to hear you talking like this, Mom."

"When God said in Genesis, 'Be fruitful and multiply . . . subdue the earth and have dominion over every living thing. . . .' He didn't intend that man be cruel or wasteful about it. When God gave us the gift of the earth, I'm sure He meant for us to cherish it, care for it and make it prosper. It's a matter of stewardship, I guess."

"What do you mean by that, Mom?"

"I believe we have a special responsibility to the earth. As we know from Genesis, the earth belongs to God. But He gave it to us as a place to live, to be nourished and to enjoy. If we aren't careful, the earth won't be capable of feeding us or giving us pleasure by its beauty. Once we use up our natural resources—our trees, our coal, our productive farmland—then what?"

Lexi was surprised to hear how much her mother had thought about this. Of course, her mother usually surprised her. Sometimes it was hard to believe that a mom could be so wise or so "with it."

"I think the church should become more active in recycling and ecology efforts," Mrs. Leighton continued. "We need to let faith and action work together.

"We should teach and encourage people not to waste, to share what they have. All of us buy more clothing than we really need and fix too much food at a meal. If we can't share our clothing and food with others, then at least we shouldn't waste it. Grandpa Carson always said that if people would just follow a few simple rules, the world could be a much nicer place to live."

"What were those rules, Mom?"

"Help people out when they need it. Give of your time as well as your money. Memorize scripture. Pray every day. Plant trees. And when you leave something behind, leave it in as good or better condition than you found it."

"That sounds pretty simple."

"It sounds simple, but if everyone did it, we'd have a much better place to live right now. We wouldn't be worrying about pollution or shortages. That was the wonderful thing about your grandfather, Lexi, he had faith that wasn't just the 'Sunday-kind-of-faith.' He lived what he believed seven days a week. Faith and life were the same thing to him."

Lexi knew lots of people who said they were Christians but only seemed to act like it on Sunday mornings. It was as if they had a hatrack beside their back door, and every morning when they went out, they picked a hat to wear. Some mornings, they picked a Christian hat. But most mornings, they'd pick a "worldly" hat. If Grandfather had had a hatrack at his back door, there would have been only one hat hanging on it.

As Lexi walked to the grocery store for her mother, it was as though her eyes had been opened for the very first time. She noticed soda pop cans and candy wrappers lying in the gutter and was shocked to see pieces of debris littering the sidewalks. Had this been here all the time? It made her sad to think how accustomed she'd become to seeing clutter on the streets.

Halfway to the market, Lexi saw a familiar figure standing on the sidewalk, staring into a store window. As she approached Minda Hannaford, Lexi took a deep breath. She could never predict what kind of mood Minda might be in—or how she'd react to whatever Lexi might say.

Fortunately, Minda was in good spirits.

"Hi, Leighton. What are you up to?"

"Grocery shopping." Lexi held up the rope bag. "How about you?"

"My closet is practically *bare*," Minda said dramatically. "I need new clothes. What do you think of that?" She pointed to a dress that looked like it had been shrink-wrapped to the mannequin.

"It's okay, but I like to be able to breath in my clothes."

Minda grinned. "Good sense of humor, Leighton. You've convinced me. I *need* that dress." Cheerfully, Minda sashayed toward the door of the boutique. With a wave, she disappeared into the store. When Lexi last saw her, Minda was gesturing broadly and pointing to the skimpy lime-green mini. Lexi hoped she wouldn't be around when Egg got a glimpse of Minda in that dress. His Adam's apple would bob so hard it might fly out of his throat!

Lexi was still grinning at the thought of the unlikely match—Egg and Minda—when she arrived at the grocery store. She quickly picked up the items she needed. When the bag boy at the check-out counter said "plastic or paper?" she held up her rope bag. "I'll have everything in this please."

The young man smiled at her. "Good idea. More people are doing that all the time."

"You don't mind?"

"Of course not. It's cheaper for the store and better for the environment. Why should anyone mind?"

Feeling better, Lexi hurried home with her purchases.

Ben met her on the front porch. His dark hair glinted in the sunlight and his beautiful almond-shaped eyes were dancing. He had a bit of news to share. "Todd called."

"He did? What did he want?"

"To talk to me," Ben said proudly. "He said, 'Hi,

little fellow, how are you?' "

Lexi suppressed a grin. "Did Todd say anything else?"

"He said that I should give Lexi a message. He said this." Ben screwed his face into a tight mask of concentration and spoke each word clearly and distinctly. " 'The clean-up starts in Cedar River Park at 1:00. Meet me by the bridge.' " Ben opened his eyes. "Was that a good message?"

"An excellent message, Ben. Thank you."

"Can I come too?" Ben looked hopeful.

Lexi understood Ben's enthusiasm, but she knew the gang could work much faster if they didn't have Ben in tow. She glanced up and down the street. A soda pop can was lying on the sidewalk.

"I've got an idea, Ben. I have a very special job for you."

When Lexi left for the river, Ben was happily carrying a bag up and down the sidewalk, picking up paper and tin cans. Lexi had a hunch that when she returned, there wouldn't be a piece of clutter or garbage anywhere.

A group had already gathered by the river, carrying garbage bags. Lexi saw Todd and the rest of the gang standing near the bridge. Binky stuck her hand in the hair and waved. "Here we are."

"Are we all just supposed to get out there and grab up garbage?" Jennifer didn't seem terribly enthused about the prospect. In fact, everyone seemed to be wondering what they were supposed to do except for Egg.

He was excited. It was apparent by the bright look in his eyes and the galloping Adam's apple at his throat. "Look at all the people who have come out to work. Isn't it great that everyone's pitching in?"

There were lots of papers, pop cans and junk lying near the river. The river itself had a dark, murky look about it. Lexi swallowed hard, trying to imagine what could turn water that ugly shade.

Just then, the mayor's voice came over a loudspeaker set up on the bridge. "I'd like to welcome you all here today to the first step in our project to clean up our beautiful river." The mayor outlined the plan that would save Cedar River from the pollution destroying it. The first wave of clean-up would be along the river, then the people were to fan into the park and the street. After the clean-up, the city would sponsor a picnic for the workers. "And, after the picnic," the mayor said with a chuckle, "I'm sure each of you will pick up your own refuse and put it in the trash cans."

Lexi, Todd, Jennifer, Binky and Egg worked side by side, trudging along the riverbank picking up refuse.

"It's incredible how much junk is lying here in this tall grass," Jennifer said. "What kind of people come down here? Pigs?"

"I seem to remember us being down here a few times, Jennifer."

"Did I ever leave a pop can or throw junk on the ground? If I did, never speak to me again."

Lexi's back was beginning to ache as she worked. She was glad that Egg had brought gloves for them because some of the trash they were picking up looked rather unappealing. She felt grubby and sweaty and could feel strands of her hair glued to her neck. Every time Lexi pushed her hair away from her face, she blackened it more with muddy streaks. It wasn't long before she could feel damp trickles of perspiration running down her back.

"Eeeekkk!!! It's gross, it's gross. Yuck!" Lexi glanced up to see Binky doing a wild dance on the grass. "It's dead. Ick, ick! Oh, no, it's alive, it's alive! Help!"

Lexi, Egg, Todd and Jennifer all dropped their bags and ran toward Binky.

"What's wrong?"

"Look at that thing. I can't pick that up."

"What is it?"

"It's dead, I know it's dead. Eeeekk! It's moving!"

They all stared down at the slimy black glob on the ground.

"Ooohh, it stinks, it stinks," Binky jumped away in disgust.

"It's only a banana peel with bugs crawling on it," Egg snorted. He picked the oozing mass up with his glove and dropped it in one of his bags. "Don't be such a baby, Binky."

"I hate bugs. I hate them. I do, I do, I do." Binky looked pale. "I thought it was something worse. Something really gross."

"I think it's all gross," Jennifer said. "I never realized how much junk was lying around. This is awful."

They were all tired, dirty and cranky. Even Egg, whose enthusiasm had been so high, looked weary. Todd looked at his watch. "It's only fifteen minutes until the picnic starts. Maybe we should get washed up at the water fountain."

"I don't think I want these hands to touch food. Not after all the filth they've picked up in the last three or four hours," Jennifer said. "People throw *everything* away. I've picked up shoes, plastic, even someone's underwear!"

"The group by the statue of the founder of Cedar River is sure enthusiastic," Lexi commented. The five elderly ladies had been bending and stooping to pick up trash with more exuberance than any other group.

"Next thing you know they'll be trying to vacuum the grass," Binky commented.

Just then, one of the ladies broke away from the group and walked toward Lexi and the gang.

"Have any of you found a gold locket?" the woman asked. Her brow wore a worried frown. "My friend Hilda lost her locket when we got here this morning and we've been trying to find it ever since."

"You mean *that's* why you've been working so hard today?" Binky gasped. "I thought you were—"

The woman blushed sheepishly. "Frankly, my friends and I just came down here to look around. We really hadn't planned to work. But when we got here and saw the mess, we could hardly go away. Besides that, Hilda lost her necklace. It seemed we were meant to stay here and clean up."

"Where was she when she lost it?"

The woman pointed to the river. "We tiptoed right along the edge next to those trees first. Then we meandered all over the park. It could be anywhere."

"I'll check the riverbank again," Egg offered. He

hurried toward the shrubs. In a moment, he began to flap his arms. "Here it is! I've found it!"

"Already? My, but he's quick."

"Good old Egg," Binky muttered as they hurried toward the bank.

Egg pointed toward the branch of a tree. "It's hanging out there. I'll bet your friend walked under the branch and the chain caught on the twigs." He eyed the slick side of the riverbank. "How did she get out so far?"

"Hilda is part nanny goat," the older woman said with a laugh. "She was looking for water-polished rocks. We never even thought to look in the branches."

Egg drew a breath and stepped down the bank's incline toward the river. The necklace dangled just out of his reach.

"If I just lean forward a little . . ." Egg squealed as his feet slid out from under him, and gave a full-fledged roar when he hit the icy water. Binky clapped her hands over her mouth not knowing if she should laugh or cry.

Egg flopped around like a rubber duck, calling, "Save me, save me, I can't swim. I'm going down for the third time. Save me!"

Workers began to run toward the spot where Egg had slipped. His cries grew louder. "Binky! Tell Mom and Dad I love them! Tell them I died for a good cause!"

With a sigh, Todd moved closer to the bank and grabbed the dangling necklace. "Egg, why don't you just stand up and walk out of the water? It's only three feet deep right here."

Shock and relief spread across Egg's red face. He quit splashing around and stood up. The water barely reached his waist. When he walked out, the group that had gathered began to clap.

"I think I'll die of embarrassment now," he said through chattering teeth.

Todd turned to give the woman her necklace.

"Thank you so much, young man," said Hilda, clutching the locket. "And thank you for trying," she whispered to the shivering Egg.

Just then, the clean-up organizer came by carrying a tray of cold drinks. "You did a great job, kids, and you're steady workers. Thanks. We really appreciate your help. Sorry you fell in, Egg. I have some dry clothes in my car. Here's the key. Why don't you change? You can return the clothes later."

It was all any of them could do to keep from laughing as Egg slunk off in the direction of the car. When he'd disappeared, they eyed the tray of beverages suspiciously. "Plastic or paper?" Jennifer asked.

"Paper, of course. Only biodegradable stuff for this group." The organizer grinned, "And there are garbage cans over there to toss them in."

"Good," Jennifer said. "If I see one more scrap of junk fall to the ground, I might lose my cool. I can't remember the last time I worked so hard."

"But the river does look better. You have to admit that," Lexi pointed out cheerfully. "Let's go sit by it while we eat our supper."

They gathered their trays of sloppy joes, chips and cake and moved toward a slight outcropping over the river. The peaceful sounds of rushing water surrounded them and for a long time, no one spoke.

It wasn't until Egg returned and began inhaling his food that the group showed signs of reviving. Todd finished his dessert and lay back on the grass, cupping his hands beneath his head and staring at the sky. "I feel better now. I think I have enough strength to get home."

"My little brother Ben was supposed to pick up all the garbage on the sidewalk in front of our house. I wonder if he's as tired as we are," Lexi said jokingly. "Knowing Ben, he's probably washed all the pebbles on the sidewalk too."

Todd leaned forward and stood up. Then he reached for Lexi's hand and pulled her up. "Come on, guys. Let's take our plates back to the trash and get going." They were almost out of the park when two boys on bicycles came peddling by. Both of them had radio headphones on and were steering their bikes with one hand and holding pop cans with the other. They tipped them up for a last swallow and flung the cans onto the grass.

"Hey you! Wait up!" Todd yelled, but the boys were oblivious to any sound other than what blared in their headphones.

Egg, tired as he was, attempted a mad dash toward the retreating bicycles. "Wait until I catch you. I'm gonna—"

"Whoa," Todd reached for Egg and held him back.

Binky darted out from behind her brother and started running after the bikes. "You come back here, you guys. I'm gonna punch your lights out. How dare you throw stuff on the ground like that. You— you litterbugs!"

When she turned around, tears of frustration and exhaustion filled her eyes. "What good is it going to do? We can pick up junk until we're blue in the face, and people like that will just throw more garbage on the ground. It's never going to do any good." She sat down and propped her face in her hands. "What's the use?"

"Don't be discouraged, Binky," Lexi said. "You're just really tired right now. We can pick up those two pop cans."

"And somebody else will drop more someplace else. It'll never change. I hate this. I wish Egg had never started telling me about pollution and ecology and recycling." Binky was about to cry.

"I'm beginning to think she's right, Lexi," Jennifer said, joining the other two girls on the grass. "So what if I recycle? My neighbors will throw away lots more than our families can ever recycle. Binky's right. What's the use?"

Lexi was tired too, but not ready to give up the fight they'd just started. "Just because everyone else isn't doing all they could doesn't mean that you shouldn't do your share. If it hadn't been for all the work we put in, those two pop cans would just be more trash on top of a huge heap. As it is, they'll be easy to pick up and recycle. What you've done today *does* make a difference. What we do every day can make a difference."

Lexi had to stop and smile. "Listen to me, I'm sounding like Egg. A couple days ago, Egg was the only one interested in the environment. I think it's catchy. You and I and our friends are interested in recycling now. Maybe it'll spread."

"The whole world is going to end up buried under a pile of clutter," Binky said morosely.

Lexi shook her head. "We don't know that. All we can do is make the place where we live better and cleaner."

"We aren't going to get people to clean up the whole town every three months," Binky said. "A lot of these people are going to lose interest. Just like me."

"I don't believe that anyone who worked here today is ever going to throw something on the sidewalk again," Lexi pointed out. "I think they're going to think about recycling. A lot of people learned that lesson today, Binky. That will make the town a better place.

"We aren't the only people in the whole world that have started to worry about our environment. If everyone in this town—in this whole country—did just one or two things like recycling cans or newspapers, things would be much better."

"That seems like so little." Binky still looked weary, but her expression was not so dejected.

"It's a start," Lexi said.

Todd threw his arm around Lexi's shoulder. "She's right. We all have to start somewhere."

"I suppose so." Binky looked off into the encroaching darkness where the bicycles had disappeared. "But if I ever catch those guys, they're going to get a piece of my mind about those pop cans. If I'd been a policeman, I think I would have arrested them!"

Suddenly, Egg, who'd been almost silent since his embarrassing tumble into the river, clapped his hands and yelled. "That's it! That's it Binky. You're a genius. That's it." Egg's eyes were glittering and a smile spread across his face. "We'll make our own police force. We'll become the environmental police!"

Chapter Six

Lexi, Todd, Binky and Jennifer stared at Egg as though he'd lost his mind.

"Maybe you'd better sit down, Egg. You look like you're going to pop a blood vessel," Todd said with a slight laugh.

Binky looked at her brother in disgust. "I think he already *has* popped one. Maybe his whole brain is gone."

Oblivious to their remarks, Egg went on, "Don't you see? It's a great idea. We'll become environmental police."

"Yeah. Right. As soon as I get through taking my exams to join the FBI and the CIA." Binky twirled her finger at her temple and rolled her eyes.

"The five of us can watch out for people who break the environmental laws like littering or not recycling glass, pop cans or newspapers. We'll look for people who waste water by placing their sprinklers so they water the sidewalks instead of the lawns."

"Right, Egg," Jennifer rejoined. "What do we do when we find one of these terrible criminals watering concrete or throwing away a newspaper? Slap them in handcuffs and drag them off to jail?"

"Of course not. We explain to them what they're doing wrong and offer to help them. I'll be collecting cans and papers for recycling this summer anyway. I can put them on my pick-up list. All people need is a little encouragement, and a reminder now and then."

"I don't get it," Binky said. "What are we supposed to tell these people? 'Hello, I'm from the Environmental Police Department and you're doing something illegal'?"

"Something like that, but you'll have to wipe the sneer off your face," Egg said pointedly. "We can explain to people that they should be reusing everything that they can. If we know of people using paper napkins or disposable diapers, we can tell them that the use of cloth napkins and cloth diapers are better for the environment.

"At the grocery store, we can encourage people to carry reusable shopping bags. Maybe we could approach the store owners and suggest they offer a few cents off the grocery bill for everyone who brings in their own bags. At the same time, we could ask them to order more recycled products—like note pads and toilet paper. If these things were more readily available, more people would use them. If people just realized they were saving trees by using sponges or cloth rags to wipe up spills instead of paper towels, that might help too."

Egg's face was getting pink again, a sure sign of his excitement. "We could start a letter-writing campaign asking store owners to sell products with less packaging. We don't need more garbage in the world. We have to ask for what we want."

"So you want the environmental police to make fools of themselves in grocery stores? Is that correct?" Binky asked sarcastically. "Somehow, I don't think that's going to keep us busy long."

"There are lots of ways to save energy."

Todd snapped his fingers. "All summer people could use their clotheslines instead of their electric dryers. That would save energy."

Jennifer smiled and wrinkled her nose. "I do love the way my sheets smell when they come off the line."

"Great point! That gives the environmental police something to go on."

"And we'd be good stewards," Lexi interjected. She'd had stewardship on her mind a lot lately, especially since the talk with her mom. Two verses: Genesis 1:1, "In the beginning God created the heavens and the earth"; and Psalm 24:1, "The earth is the Lord's and everything in it," had been rattling around in her brain for days. Surely God didn't want to see His beautiful earth turned into a junk pile!

Often Lexi thought of herself as being too young and inexperienced to do anything really significant in the Lord's work, but here was something that was truly important for all of mankind. God was giving her and her friends an opportunity for service.

Sometimes Lexi felt God spoke to her in a very personal way. She sensed it happening again. He was giving her the go-ahead to encourage Egg in his environmental project—even in his campaign to put a brick in every toilet!

Lexi giggled.

"Now what?" Todd said with a half smile. "Something you should share with us?"

It was Lexi's turn to blush. "I just had the most bizarre thought."

"You'd better explain yourself," Jennifer said. "I'm curious."

"Here we are, having this strange conversation about people using sponges instead of paper towels, putting bricks in their toilets and encouraging mothers to quit using disposable diapers . . ."

"Go on, don't stop now."

"And I feel like God just spoke to me."

Egg's eyes grew wide. "What did He say?" Egg was always fascinated by Lexi's personal relationship with the Lord.

"I think He's saying, 'Go for it.' I don't think He likes the earth being trashed anymore than we do. This is one area in which teenagers can make a difference. If we let people know that we're doing this ecology thing for the right reasons, because this planet is a gift from God, so much the better. It's a gift that should be preserved and cherished. We can clean up the planet and get out the message about God's generosity at the same time. *That's* what I was giggling about."

"You are one strange cookie," Egg said to Lexi. His long, thin face broke into a grin. "But I have to agree with you. God doesn't talk to me like He talks to you, but this time I really like what He has to say."

"You always like anyone who agrees with you, Egg," Binky said, but she, too, had an interested light in her eyes.

Lexi realized that although Egg and Binky didn't

know God the way she did, they were growing closer and closer to that moment when they would invite Him into their lives. Seeing that was like watching a rose unfold, petal by petal, until it opened to its most beautiful blossom.

"So? What do you think?" Egg looked hopefully around to his friends.

"Well, if Lexi feels the Lord is really in this, then I'm all for it," Todd said.

"I can accept that," Jennifer said. "But, I don't know about this 'environmental police' bit. That sounds awfully hokey to me."

Egg looked insulted as his sister nodded emphatically and added, "Egg always has these bizarre ideas . . ."

"We aren't going to be wearing badges or anything," Lexi interjected. "It's not a bad concept. We'll just watch for the things that we've talked about and make a point of showing people ways to do things that will be less harmful to the environment. How does that sound?"

Lexi had a hunch that what Egg *really* wanted was to work up some kind of badge or uniform that said "environmental police." She also knew that Egg would be the only one willing to make himself conspicuous. Their plan would work more effectively this way—quietly—one to one, spreading the message about saving the environment.

"Next time we get together," Lexi suggested, "we can tell each other what kind of progress we've made."

The others began to talk at once. Lexi glanced up to see Anna Marie Arnold walking by. Quietly she excused herself.

"Hi, Anna Marie. How are you?" Lexi's gaze took in Anna Marie's thin figure.

"Fine, Lexi. What are you guys up to?"

Lexi explained Egg's idea about the environmental police.

"I think it's a great idea," responded Anna Marie enthusiastically.

"Then consider yourself one of us," Lexi said. She threw her arm around Anna Marie's thin shoulders and gave her a squeeze. "Where are you going?"

"Home. Do you want to walk with me?"

Lexi caught Todd's eye. He nodded and waved her on. Todd understood. They'd all been worried about Anna Marie lately.

As the girls walked, they discussed the environmental issues that were on everyone's mind, including Egg's zany idea to put a brick in every toilet. Finally, when the conversation waned, Lexi asked Anna Marie again how she'd been lately.

"Oh, I've been just fine."

"How are you *really*, Anna Marie? You look *awfully* thin to me." *Thinner than ever,* Lexi thought to herself.

"This anorexia thing has been a real battle, Lexi. I didn't know how hard it would be. You'd think after all these weeks and months of therapy I'd have things straightened out in my head. I think I'm finally getting there, though." Anna Marie sighed. "I don't see the therapist quite as often anymore. I *am* eating more and feeling stronger."

"That's good. I'm glad to hear it."

"My therapist made me sign a contract stating that I would eat at every meal. I don't always eat much, but I do sit down to the table and have something. Actually, I think I've gained a couple pounds." Anna Marie stopped and leaned against a brick wall. "The therapist and my family both feel that the therapy is finally starting to work. I'm facing up to some of the things that made me feel so out of control before.

"I told the therapist about the competition I felt with my sister and the pressure I felt to please my father. He said that was typical of anoretic patients." Anna Marie smiled shyly. "Once I started telling him about all the things that bothered me—grades, popularity, boys—he told me he could have predicted all those things. I suppose I should have known most teenagers worry about those kinds of things. My personality just tends to take it all to the extreme.

"I worry about every grade. Sometimes I find myself studying and restudying a subject until I practically memorize the chapter. Then I come home from school afraid that I've flunked the test. I used to be that way about boys, too. I always felt I failed when it came to them. I knew I wasn't popular and never would be. And I believed my weight was at the root of it all." A smile softened Anna Marie's expression. "My friendship with Egg has helped me a lot."

"Oh? In what way?" Lexi felt the warmth of the brick wall seeping into her back.

"My friendship with Egg has made me realize that girls and boys can be good friends. He's also made me realize that I don't have to have a 'boyfriend.' Having a friend who's a boy is just as nice and not nearly so worrisome. My friendships with Egg, Todd and Harry Cramer have made me realize that I *am* likeable to the opposite sex after all. Someday, the right one for me will come along."

"It seems strange to me that those things bring on anorexia," Lexi commented softly.

"My therapist says I have a 'compulsive personality.' That means that everything is either all-or-none with me. When I decided I wanted complete control of my body, I went to extremes that normal people wouldn't attempt."

The girls began to walk again, more slowly than before.

"The emotions I feel when I'm around food may never completely go away, but I'm on top of it for now."

"Will you be able to quit seeing the doctor?" Lexi asked. Anna Marie shook her head. "Not for a while. Anorexia isn't a problem that I can tie up with a neat little bow and put away. I have to stay mentally healthy." Anna Marie looked at Lexi thoughtfully. "You've helped me, you know."

"I have?" Lexi was surprised.

"You're the most mentally healthy person I know," Anna Marie said frankly. "I've often wondered what it is about you that's different from the other kids I know. Finally I decided it was the Christianity thing. You really believe what the Bible has to say.

"Our family has started going to church. It's hard to get in the habit when you've been accustomed to sleeping in on Sunday mornings, but we go more regularly now. I think it's helping.

"My dad says that church is the one place in the world that accepts everyone," Lexi said. "That's why churches are filled with so many kinds of people, both those who are spiritually healthy and those who are still seeking."

"I do think it's fun," Anna Marie said. "I wish our church had a youth group, though. There are activities for the little kids and for the young marrieds. The one big lack is something for the teenagers. Maybe they think it's too hard to compete with school activities and other things young people become involved in. Maybe someday . . ."

That was something Lexi would have to think about. She was surprised to hear of a church who didn't have their own youth group.

———————

"Did you have a nice talk with Anna Marie?" Jennifer asked, her voice clear and lazy over the telephone line.

"Yes. She said she's going to church now with her family. But her church doesn't even have a youth group."

"Bor-ing!" Jennifer exclaimed. "Everyone needs to have a little fun. That is, except for remedial students."

Lexi caught on immediately, "Summer school's tough, huh?"

"Tough!" Jennifer groaned. "You can't imagine it. I wish I didn't have to go." Jennifer had kept her dyslexia a secret until just a year ago. "It's a real drag to be in school when everyone else is out having a good time."

"Right. I'm having a good time cleaning puppy cages. Todd's having a marvelous time working in his brother's garage. Egg's having a great time collecting sticky pop cans. Are you *sure* you're envious?"

"Well, when you put it that way . . . No, school is still a drag. After all, this *is* summer vacation."

True. It *was* summer vacation—and stacking up to be a very interesting one at that.

Chapter Seven

"Run a sponge over that fender, Lexi," Todd instructed as he rinsed the hood of his hulking '49 Ford.

They'd parked the car on the Leighton driveway and were giving it a thorough cleaning. Mr. Leighton was in the backyard singing over the sound of the lawnmower. Ben was washing the sidewalk. The sun was warm and bright, and Lexi could hear the birds chirping their approval in the nearby trees.

"Hello there!" Todd and Lexi turned as Binky tramped toward them. "This looks like a busy place."

Todd kicked the wheel of the old car. "Looks better, doesn't she?"

It was obvious to Lexi that her friend was preoccupied. "You don't look very happy, Binky."

Binky stared at Ben as he hosed down the sidewalk. "Well, I don't want to be a nag or anything."

Todd leaned against the car's fender. "There's something you want to say and you'll burst if you don't get it out. What is it?"

"Maybe it's living with Egg."

"What's Egg got to do with it, Binky?"

Binky pointed at the running hose lying on the sidewalk. "You're wasting water."

"But we're washing the car. We have to use water."

"You could use buckets. And you could turn off the hose when you're not using it."

Todd and Lexi looked guiltily at each other. Binky was right. They'd poured a lot of water onto the sidewalk as they'd scrubbed the car. "Well, at least we watered a lot of grass while we worked," Lexi joked weakly.

"You shouldn't be watering the grass in the middle of the day when most evaporation takes place. Dad says if you water in the morning or at night, it does more good." Binky was taking this environmental police thing very seriously. "And what's he doing?" Binky pointed to Ben as he happily washed the sidewalk.

"We just wanted to keep him busy," Lexi admitted. "The sidewalk was awfully dirty in front of the house." Even as she said it, she realized what a waste it was to occupy her little brother in such a way.

"And about your dad," Binky said.

Todd and Lexi both blinked. What had Mr. Leighton done?

"He's cutting the grass awfully short, isn't he?"

"That's what it's all about, Binky."

"That's not what I mean. Dad says if you cut the grass a little longer, it'll hold more moisture and give the roots more shade. Then you don't have to water as often."

"You're right on all counts, Binky. We're sorry." Todd gave a twist on the hose and turned it off. "No more running water unless we're using it."

Silently, Lexi went into the garage and came back

with a broom. "Ben," she called. "You can quit hosing the sidewalk now. Just sweep it. It'll get the dirt off fine, and you won't waste any water."

Todd headed for the backyard. "I'll remind Mr. Leighton to raise the blade on the lawnmower."

While Todd was gone, Lexi pointed to some buckets her mother had placed under the rainspouts around the house. "We're not completely delinquent. My mother is saving rain water to use for her plants."

"Sorry if I sounded like an old ogre, but when you live with Egg for a while . . ." she shrugged her shoulders, "well, you can about imagine."

When Egg got an idea in his head, there was no stopping him. Sometimes—like now, that personality trait worked for good. However, Egg's single-mindedness could also get him into trouble.

"Binky, why don't you and Todd come inside and have a glass of lemonade?"

"Sounds good to me." Todd wiped beads of perspiration from his forehead. "It's hot out here."

"Me too," Binky said. "Being an environmental policewoman is tough work." Her quirky smile made Todd and Lexi laugh.

Lexi poured three tall glasses of lemonade and searched the canisters until she found a stash of chocolate chip cookies.

"Hi, kids. Are you done with your chores?" Mrs. Leighton entered the kitchen.

"Mom, when you were young, did people ever talk about saving energy or saving water?"

"Not really. The world was a pretty extravagant place, I guess. We didn't realize that our resources could run out. We took for granted that there'd be enough for all of us for as long as we wanted." A gentle smile spread over Mrs. Leighton's face. "Although I didn't realize it at the time, I did a little conserving of my own."

"Oh? How was that?"

"When you and Ben were little, I never watered the grass until the two of you were driving me absolutely crazy."

"How did that help?" Binky asked.

"When the kids got too much for me, I'd ask them if they wanted to play in the sprinkler. I'd do my yard work and water the lawn while Lexi and Ben had their fun. Pretty smart, huh?"

Mrs. Leighton winked at Binky.

"I'll have to tell Egg about that one!"

Suddenly Binky changed the subject, "Have you heard when Peggy Madison will be coming home? I really miss her."

"I've been wondering myself," Todd admitted.

Binky didn't know that Peggy had left Cedar River because she was pregnant, and Lexi didn't want to spill her secret.

"Frankly, I think it's odd that Peggy isn't already back," Binky said with a puzzled expression. "School's out. I thought she was going to finish the school year in Arizona and come home."

Lexi was relieved to hear the telephone ring.

"Lexi? Is that you?" The familiar voice sounded distant. "It's Peggy, Lexi. Don't you recognize my voice?"

Lexi's heart skipped a beat. It had been months since she'd talked to her friend. "Peggy! Where are you?"

"I'm still in Arizona. I'm calling from my uncle's house."

"It's great to hear you," Lexi said with enthusiasm. "How are you?"

There was a long pause at the other end of the line. "I'm all right, Lexi. Not great, but not awful."

Peggy sounded different. Older, nervous. "I'm coming home, Lexi. I'll be arriving in Cedar River on Monday afternoon."

That was only two days away.

"How is everyone, Lexi?" Peggy asked.

"Todd and Binky are here with me in the kitchen. They're just great. Todd and I were washing his old car. Do you remember the old Ford? It hasn't changed a bit."

"Does anyone know?" Peggy asked urgently. "About the baby, I mean?"

Lexi held the telephone close to her ear so that Peggy's voice would not project into the room. "Not that I know of," Lexi said softly. "I haven't said anything. Listen, Peggy. Everything's going to be fine. We're all looking forward to seeing you." Lexi chose her words carefully, wanting to comfort her friend without giving away the secret that she'd so diligently kept.

"Have you seen Chad?" Peggy's voice quivered as it hung on the name.

"Not a lot, Peggy. Chad stays pretty much to himself." He'd been quiet, withdrawn and depressed since Peggy had left.

Ben chose that moment to burst into the kitchen, his dark eyes frantic. "My bunny escaped!" he said, flapping his arms wildly. "Help me catch it!"

"Come on, little fellow." Todd took Ben's hand. "Your sister's on the phone. Binky and I will catch your bunny for you."

Binky slid off her stool and raced after the two boys, leaving Lexi alone in the kitchen.

"What was that commotion?" Peggy asked.

"Ben's rabbit escaped. Todd and Binky went to help him catch it. Now we can talk."

"I thought you were sounding a little funny," Peggy said, "like there were things you couldn't say."

"Binky doesn't know about your baby," Lexi admitted. "I didn't want to let the secret out."

"Thanks. I appreciate it. It's going to be hard enough coming back without having the whole world know that I've had a child."

Peggy's voice quivered with emotion. "Chad writes to me a couple times a week, but I've only answered a few of his letters," Peggy admitted. "I didn't know what to say, Lexi. What do you say to the boy who's the father of your child? The child you gave up for adoption?"

"I . . . I don't know," Lexi stammered.

"He wants to act like this thing never happened between us. That I wasn't forced to go away to live with my uncle." Peggy's voice took on a bitter edge. "He wants to pretend everything's just the same, Lexi. But it's not. *I'm* not the same. How can I face him? How can I face anyone?" Lexi could hear her friend's tears.

"You don't have to worry about facing Todd or me," Lexi assured her, feeling her own tears surfacing. "We know your secret. And you're still our friend."

A long, powerful silence filled the line. "Thank you, I knew I could count on you." Peggy's voice was again remote and distant. "Well, I just wanted you to know that I'd be back in Cedar River on Monday."

"I'm looking forward to seeing you, Peggy. I've missed you." There was a quiet click at the other end of the line. Lexi stared at the receiver. Peggy had changed. Lexi felt a small tremor in the pit of her stomach.

Sudden squealing and screaming in the back yard sent Lexi dashing for the back door. Ben, Mr. Leighton, Todd and Binky were all trying to corner the tiny pet rabbit that managed to escape all of them. Lexi watched the comical circus for a moment before she stepped back into the kitchen.

When Lexi returned to the yard, she held a large fresh carrot with a sprouting of greens on the top. She sat down in the middle of the yard and held the carrot out in front of her. The greens caught the bunny's attention. His nose twitched to the right and left. In a moment he hopped toward the treat and Ben was able to capture him in his arms.

"You're so smart, Lexi," Ben crowed. "You helped me catch my bunny."

"I've done it before, you know," Lexi said with a laugh. "When are you going to learn that bunny gets frightened when he's being chased?"

"Daddy and Todd and Binky were chasing too," Ben pointed out.

"You'll have to spend more time with that bunny, Ben. Pet him and make him tame so he doesn't hop away whenever he gets out of his cage."

"Well, that was exciting," Todd said as he joined Lexi on the grass.

Binky flung herself down beside them. "What did Peggy have to say? When's she coming home?"

"She'll be here on Monday."

Binky clapped her hands together and squealed with delight. "Isn't that great?" She snapped her fingers. "I know what we should do. We should have a welcome home party for Peggy."

"Binky, I'm not sure that's a good idea."

"Of course it is. It's a great idea. Peggy's one of our best friends and she's been away for a long time. We want to hear how it was going to school in Arizona. Besides, she'll have to catch up on all the news that's been happening here. I think a party is a wonderful idea, don't you, Todd?"

"Ah, well, maybe. Sure, why not?" Todd stammered. He shrugged his shoulders helplessly when Lexi gave him a sharp glance.

"Peggy might not want a party right away, Binky."

"Why wouldn't she? Why wouldn't *anyone* want a party?"

"She might be tired, you know. She sounded that way on the telephone. And," Lexi added, "she might want to spend a little time alone with Chad."

"Oh, Chad." Binky's face fell. "That's the one big mystery. I can't understand why Peggy went away and left him behind. They were as thick as thieves."

"Maybe we'd better not rush Peggy with this party. Why don't you let me talk to her first? I'll ask her if she thinks it would be a good idea."

"Then it wouldn't be a surprise!"

"That would be all right. Let's give her a couple days to rest up." Lexi was trying to buy time. She wanted to be sure that Peggy wouldn't be upset by seeing so many of her old friends at once.

"I suppose, but I like the idea of a surprise party much better."

"Trust me on this one, Bink," Lexi said. "It's going to be emotional to come home. Let's give her a couple of days and then, if she wants it, we can have a really nice party."

Fortunately Lexi's mother came to the kitchen doorway at that moment. "Binky, your mother's on the phone. She wants you to come home now."

Binky stood up reluctantly. "Guess I have to leave. I can hardly wait to get home and tell Egg that Peggy's coming back." She pointed a finger at Lexi. "Don't forget about that party. I think it's important that we have one. Thanks for the lemonade and cookies. See you tomorrow."

Lexi and Todd were silent until Binky was out of sight.

"Do you think something's wrong with Peggy?" Todd asked.

"I'm not sure," Lexi admitted.

"What did she sound like?"

"Bad, Todd. She sounded sad, nervous, angry and . . . scared. Really scared."

"I'd be scared too if I were her," Todd said bluntly. "She doesn't know how far her secret has spread or what people think of her. Besides that, she's going to have a tough time seeing Chad."

"Do you think so?" Lexi asked. "They acted like they were so much in love."

"I can only speak from a guy's perspective, Lexi, but if I were going to see a girl who'd been pregnant with my baby and given it up, I'd be pretty emotional."

"I never thought about it that way. I guess I've always thought of it from Peggy's viewpoint, not Chad's."

"Unwed fathers can have a tough time, too. They don't have to pay the physical price, but I'm sure there's a big emotional one. For the rest of his life, Chad's going to wonder about that baby. What it looked like. Who it is. Where it lives. Who its adoptive parents are. For the rest of his life he's going to look at kids that are the same age as that child and he'll wonder, 'Are you the one? Are you mine?' Someday he might read about a celebrity in a magazine or a newspaper and see a picture that reminds him of himself or of Peggy. He'll wonder, 'Is that my child?' And he'll never know."

All of what Todd said made a great deal of sense. No wonder Peggy was nervous and Chad so withdrawn! There was much more to their problem than Lexi could even imagine.

"At least I talked Binky out of having a party on Monday night."

"If you don't have the party, what will we tell the gang? They'll be suspicious that something is wrong. Talk to Peggy, Lexi. Get an idea about how she's feeling. You're one of her very best friends."

"I *was* one of her very best friends, Todd. I don't know anymore. Peggy's had an experience that I can't even begin to understand. I really don't know if we're friends anymore."

She'd put into words the fear she'd been harboring. Could her relationship with Peggy withstand the traumatic separation they'd experienced? Had she lost her friend for good or was her friend finally coming home?

That evening, after Todd had gone and Ben had been tucked into bed, Lexi went to her room. She closed the door and fell to her knees. With her face cupped in her hands, she began to pray.

"Oh, Father. Take care of Peggy. Bring her home safely. Help her to know that I'm her friend no matter what. Help her to deal with Chad, her parents and the kids at school. She's not very old to have all these problems, God. Be her strength. I ask this in Jesus' name. Amen."

Though Lexi crawled into bed and turned out the light, it was a long time before she slept.

One disturbing question kept creeping into her mind. Would she and Peggy still be friends? Or had life unalterably changed for them both?

Chapter Eight

Monday, Binky arrived after lunch while Lexi was doing the dishes.

Ben was at the kitchen table drawing pictures of his rabbit. "Hi, Binky," he said. "My bunny's okay. He hasn't gotten out of his house for days."

"I'm glad to hear that, Ben." Binky ruffled the little boy's dark silky hair. "I'm not in the mood to chase a rabbit today."

"I'm making him tame, Binky. He's eaten three carrots."

"Don't feed him anymore," Lexi said patiently. "That poor bunny is going to get a tummyache."

"Now what are you doing?" Lexi asked as Binky poked her nose into the kitchen sink.

"Are you planning to use the dishwasher? Automatic dishwashers can use as many as twenty-five gallons of water."

Lexi opened the dishwasher to show the empty interior. "I'm washing them all by hand, Binky, in this basin. I turn off the tap water every time I'm done rinsing a dish and I never let it run. And," Lexi said, holding up a pitcher of clear water, "I'm going to put this in the refrigerator so that nobody in the family has to run tap water to get a cold drink."

Binky smiled her approval. "Very good, Lexi. You're catching on."

"I am grateful that I don't live with you and Egg. You two would drive me crazy."

"Hey, I'm an environmental policewoman. It's a dirty job, but somebody's gotta do it."

Ben lost interest in the picture he was drawing. "How can *I* help save water, Binky?" he inquired.

"Lots of ways, Ben. You'd be a truly excellent environmental policeman."

Ben's eyes grew wide. "I would? What could I do?"

Oh, oh, Lexi thought to herself. *Here goes the last peaceful moment in the Leighton household.*

"Make sure everyone in your house takes really quick showers. Showers use a lot of water every minute. If somebody takes a bath in the tub, make sure they don't fill the tub to the top. All they need is enough water for them to get clean."

Ben nodded, listening intently.

"When you brush your teeth, don't let the tap water run. Turn it on only to rinse out your brush."

"Ben can do that," Ben announced.

"And when you wash your hands, Ben," Binky said, "put the stopper in the basin. Don't keep running the water until you're all done washing your hands. You can rinse your hands in the water that's in the basin. That will save a gallon of water. Another thing you can do is remind your mother to wash only full loads of clothes. She shouldn't waste water by just throwing one or two things in the wash at a time."

Ben's expression was intent. "I can do all that. I

can be an environmental policeman." He had a difficult time pronouncing environmental. "Do I get a badge?"

Binky picked up a piece of Ben's drawing paper. "May I use this, Ben?"

He nodded solemnly.

Binky drew a big red badge on the paper. With other markers, she lettered the words "Environmental Police: Benjamin Leighton." "There's your badge, Ben. You can hang it on the wall or cut it out and wear it on your shirt."

"Look, Lexi. I'm a policeman," Ben said proudly. "I'm somebody."

Lexi grabbed her little brother by the shoulders. "You've always been somebody, Ben. Somebody very special."

"Now I have a badge."

"Go show it to Mom, Ben," Lexi said. "You'd better warn her what environmental policemen do, so she isn't surprised later on."

"I'll make sure she's not wasting water." Ben disappeared through the kitchen door.

Lexi shook her head at Binky. "Now my house will be just as crazy as yours. With Egg and Ben looking out for the environment, neither of us are going to get any rest."

"I know. Isn't it wonderful?" Binky grinned menacingly. "Now I'm not the only one."

Lexi pointed an accusing finger at Binky. "You did that on purpose."

"Who me?" The girls laughed together.

"Have you heard from her?" Binky asked. "Has Peggy called?"

"Not yet. Her plane arrives later this evening."

"It'll be so great to see her again," Binky said. "I can hardly wait."

Tonight was the night Lexi had been waiting for. Peggy would be home again at last.

After supper, Lexi sat on the porch reading her Bible. She'd felt restless all afternoon. When intangible things were troubling her, Lexi liked to read from the Psalms. The beautiful poetry was calming. Tonight, Lexi read Psalm 100.

Shout for joy to the Lord, all the earth. Worship the Lord with gladness; come before him with joyful songs. Know that the Lord is God. It is he who has made us, and we are his; we are his people, the sheep of his pasture. Enter his gates with thanksgiving and his courts with praise; give thanks to him and praise his name. For the Lord is good and his love endures forever; his faithfulness continues through all generations.

Lexi liked that. *Know that the Lord is God.* That He made us and we are His. No matter what else happened, the Lord promised to love her and everyone of His children—that meant Peggy, too.

Peggy was in Cedar River by now, Lexi mused. She lived only a few houses away. Lexi peered down the street. Perhaps she'd get a glimpse of her if . . . Lexi drew in a sharp breath. Peggy Madison was coming down the street, looking the same as always!

Peggy's thick red hair glinted in the waning light and Lexi could imagine the sprinkling of freckles across her short nose. She wore navy blue shorts and a pale blue blouse. Her hair was longer now, otherwise, she seemed the same.

"Peggy!" Lexi raced down the steps toward the sidewalk. They met at the front gate, hugging, squealing, laughing, crying.

"You look wonderful."

"So do you. You haven't changed a bit. But your hair is longer."

"Yours too. I love it that way."

Slowly the girls made their way to the Leighton's front porch.

"Sit down. I was reading."

Peggy noticed the Bible, but didn't comment on it. Instead, she lowered herself into a chair and stared expectantly at Lexi.

Lexi didn't know what to say. Peggy was the same, and yet, she was entirely different.

"Did you have a good trip?" Lexi asked.

"Yes."

"I like flying, don't you?"

"Yes," Peggy said again.

A long silence hung between them. Lexi could sense that Peggy wanted to talk about things far more serious than airplane rides. "A lot has happened since we saw each other last, hasn't it?"

Peggy eyes filled with sudden tears.

"Did you know that my grandfather died?"

"No, Lexi, I didn't."

"It was tough, really tough. My Grandmother Carson came to live with us for a while."

"Is she still here?" Peggy wondered.

"No, we had to put her in a nursing home. She has Alzheimer's disease."

"I'm so sorry," Peggy said, her voice full of sympathy. "I had no idea."

"I didn't think so. It was difficult for me to write about it," Lexi admitted. "And our letters weren't exactly steady."

"I wasn't always in the mood for writing," Peggy admitted. "I really am sorry about your grandparents, Lexi." Peggy stared for a long moment at the Bible. "Same old Lexi. Still reading Bible verses."

Lexi took Peggy's hand in her own and stared directly into her friend's eyes. "How are you, Peggy? How are you *really*?"

That one simple question opened the doorway to a flood of emotions, of feelings, of tears.

"I'm empty, Lexi. That's how I am. Empty." Peggy's hands moved across her flat stomach. "I can't explain how I feel any other way. I spent nine months being pregnant, having a baby grow inside me. For nine months I knew it was there. The last few months, I could feel it kick, roll and hiccup. I went to the doctor and heard its heartbeat. At night, when I wanted to sleep, the baby would become restless. It would kick and squirm and keep me awake. Now that baby is gone, Lexi. I gave it away. That beautiful baby that had been mine for all those months is gone."

Peggy's hands clenched and unclenched over her abdomen. "I feel empty, Lexi. I *am* empty. The baby is gone. Gone from my body and gone from my life."

Lexi ached for her friend, but didn't know what to say. Childbirth was beyond her experience.

"I've spent the last nine months of my life being scared, Lexi. Scared of being pregnant. Scared of what was happening to me. Scared of what was going to happen to my baby. The night I went into labor, I was so confused, I wished I could die."

Lexi remained silent, listening intently.

"I didn't know what giving birth was going to be like. I'd heard all kinds of horror stories about the pain and the long hours it took to deliver a baby. I didn't want to go through that. Yet, at the same time, I knew that after that night I wouldn't be pregnant any longer. I could finally get on with my life. I thought that would be the worst night of my life, but it wasn't." The tears were running freely down Peggy's cheeks now. "Do you know what the worst night was?"

Lexi shook her head.

"The night I gave my baby up for adoption."

"Peggy, you don't have to tell me this."

"I want to, Lexi. I haven't been able to talk to anyone my own age for months. You're the only one who knew I was pregnant. I know you can keep a secret. I need to talk to someone. I was so stupid. I actually believed that once I gave the baby up for adoption I would be happy, that my troubles would be over and I could go back to school and everything would be the same. Once I signed the papers, I realized that wasn't true at all. There's no way you can go back. There's no way to undo what I've done. There's no way to forget that I held my baby in my arms. I've never felt so empty in my entire life."

Lexi's chest hurt. She felt as if her heart were breaking for her friend. Peggy buried her face in her hands and sobbed. "If I'd known what I was going to go through before this was over, I *never* would have slept with Chad. Never." Peggy looked up, her cheeks tearstained. "It's not worth it, Lexi. Nothing is worth this kind of pain. No boy is worth it. No relationship is worth it. I understand now why sex is meant for marriage. Because babies are meant to be kept and loved by *two* parents. I couldn't do that, Lexi. I had to give my baby up." Peggy stared at Lexi intently. "I don't know about your relationship with Todd, but trust me on this one, Lexi, never let happen to you what's happened to me."

Lexi took Peggy's hand in her own and held it tightly. At the same time, she sent a battery of prayers to God begging, pleading with Him to help her, to give her the right words, to show her what she should do and say.

Nearly five minutes passed before Peggy spoke again. "Good old Lexi. Always right there. Always a friend."

Lexi wiped a tear from Peggy's cheek. "I want to be your friend, Peggy. Right now I don't know what to say."

Peggy snuffled back her tears. "That's all right, Lexi. You don't have to say anything. You've said things in the past that helped me enough.

"You're the one that talked to me about God." Peggy continued. "You're the one who told me how much this baby and I meant to Him. You're the one who convinced me to talk to my parents when I got pregnant. When things got really bad, I'd go to the Bible—to Psalm 139—and read the part about a baby being formed inside its mother.

For you created my inmost being; you knit me
together in my mother's womb. I praise you because I am fearfully and wonderfully made. . . .
When I was woven together in the depths of the
earth, your eyes saw my unformed body. All the
days ordained for me were written in your book
before one of them came to be.

"Every time I read those verses, I realized how
special this baby was to God and how special I was
to Him, too. It kept me going."

How God had blessed the words He'd given her!
Lexi was awed to think of it.

Peggy smiled at the expression on Lexi's face.
"Hey, I don't want to make you cry, too."

Lexi sniffed back the tears. "I think it's too late,
Peggy."

The girls sat with their arms around each other
until they regained their composure.

"There's a little bit of hope in this," Peggy said.
"Maybe someday, my baby will find the letter."

"What letter?" Lexi asked, wiping away a tear.

"I wrote a letter to my baby and put it in the
adoption file," Peggy explained. "I told her about myself and Chad and what happened to us. I told her
how young we were and why I decided it was best to
give her up for adoption rather than try to raise her
or to have an abortion. I wanted her to understand
that I did it out of love. She shouldn't feel unloved
because she was given away, but loved even more
than other babies are. Someday, maybe she'll check
into her file and find that letter."

"Do you think you'd like to have your child look
for you someday?" Lexi asked. She'd read about chil-

dren who'd looked for their biological parents when
they were grown.

"I think so. My uncle and I talked about that. He
said I should never keep this baby a secret from the
man I marry. If she were to look me up someday and
I hadn't told my husband about my past, it could be
very hard for everyone." Peggy seemed dumbfounded
by her predicament. "I never dreamed how compli-
cated things could be."

A weak smile flitted across her face. "They tell
me my baby is getting wonderful parents. Her dad's
a minister and her adoptive mom is a teacher. That
means she's going to know God. Isn't that great,
Lexi? I hope she's smart and pretty and has a wonderful life.

"She has red hair, Lexi, just like me." Peggy
rested her head in her palm. "It feels weird being
back here," she said matter-of-factly. "Here I am,
trying to act like nothing ever happened and my
whole life has changed completely."

"Have you seen anyone else yet?"

"You mean Chad?" Peggy went right to the point.
"No. I don't want to see Chad. Not now. Not yet."

"What's going to happen with you two? Is it over
between you?"

"Chad wants to pick up where we left off," Peggy
admitted.

"Will you?"

Peggy shook her head so firmly that her red hair
swung at her shoulders. "No. We can't pick up where
we left off. Chad and I got ourselves into too much
trouble to let that happen again. The next time I
have an intimate relationship with a man it's going

to be my husband. Chad thinks we can ignore the past nine months and go back to being the two teen-agers that we were before. I don't feel like a teenager anymore, Lexi. Some days I feel like I'm a hundred years old. I won't give that part of me to Chad again. Never."

A look of regret flitted across Peggy's features. "One of the things I feel most badly about, Lexi, is that I didn't save that part of myself for marriage. Kids aren't supposed to have sex with one another. I've always heard that. Now I know why. I'm sorry I had to learn it for myself. We aren't ready. Not phys-ically, not emotionally, not in any way. Now I've lost something that I would have liked to take into my marriage. I won't make the same mistake twice."

"So you won't date Chad anymore?"

Peggy shrugged her shoulders. "I don't know what to do about Chad. I still love him, Lexi. I really do. Perhaps I'll just have to wait and see what Chad says when we're together. But, my guess is that he hasn't grown up and changed like I have in the past few months."

Lexi thought about the times she'd seen Chad Allen recently. He was usually alone, always quiet. He appeared to be waiting for Peggy to come home and renew their relationship.

Suddenly the screen door clattered and Ben came out of the house, carrying a bucket of water for the planters on the porch. "Hi, Peggy," Ben said. He set his water bucket down and grabbed Peggy's face be-tween his hands and squeezed. "You're still pretty."

"And you're still charming, Benjamin Leighton," Peggy said. She gave Ben a hug. "Oh, Ben, I've missed you. You're as cuddly as ever."

"I'm a policeman," Ben said.

"You are? Is that the game you're playing today?"

"It's no game." Ben pointed at the bucket of water. "I'm an envi-ron-mental policeman."

"It's Egg's latest scheme," Lexi explained. "We've been having a problem with pollution in Cedar River lately. Egg has decided that if teenagers will pitch in and help, we could do a lot to improve the environment." Lexi explained the idea behind the environmental policemen and Egg's campaign to get everyone to recycle and conserve energy. By the time she was done, Peggy was laughing.

"So you have a big recycling and 'save water' campaign going on," Peggy said happily. "Sounds just like my friends. Always up to something, trying to do some good for someone."

Lexi was delighted to see the new brightness on Peggy's face.

"All of a sudden, I'm anxious to see the rest of my friends," she admitted.

"I practically had to tie Binky down," Lexi said. "She wanted to have a party for you tonight, but I told her that I thought we should wait and see how you felt about it."

"Well, I would like to see my friends," Peggy said again. "But I don't know, a party is a lot of trouble—"

"It's no trouble at all," Lexi assured her. "Binky will be more than happy to help me. She was angry with me for putting it off.

"It might be easier if we have a party," Lexi continued. "There will be so much commotion and activity that no one will have an opportunity to ask you any really difficult questions. We could have as many or as few guests as you'd like."

"Just a few," Peggy said. "I think I'd better start small."

Lexi reached for the notebook and pencil she always kept with her Bible. "Tell me who you want to see. I'll write the guest list and we'll have this party organized in no time. There's Todd, of course, and Egg, Binky and Jennifer Golden. We could have some of the girls' basketball team if you'd like. Would you mind if I invited Harry Cramer?" Lexi wondered.

"Harry. Isn't he that good-looking senior boy?"

"He and Binky spent a lot of time together this winter. Binky would be disappointed if he weren't invited."

"It will be nice to have some kids around that I don't know very well. I'll trust you, Lexi. I'm sure you'll plan a great party." Peggy stood to leave.

Lexi walked her friend to the gate. Impulsively, Peggy threw her arms around Lexi's shoulders and gave her a hug.

"It is so good to see you, Lexi." Peggy's voice trailed away for a moment. "Were you praying for me?"

"Every day," Lexi admitted. "Morning and night. And sometimes even during study hall."

"I really did sense that God was near me, giving me strength and courage. I appreciate your prayers, Lexi. Thank you."

As Lexi watched her friend walk away she sensed that Peggy needed her prayers now more than ever.

Chapter Nine

"Do you think we have enough soda?"

"Where did you put the napkins?"

"I've looked in the refrigerator three times and I can't find the pepperoni."

"Are you sure Todd brought enough ice cream?"

"Egg was in charge of the chocolate sauce and it's probably sitting on a counter somewhere right now."

"Here's the chocolate sauce," Lexi said holding up a paper bag. "Calm down, Binky. Everything's going to be fine."

"Oh, I love a party, don't you?" Binky said with a squeal. "Do you think we've forgotten anything?"

"I don't see how we could have," Lexi said with a laugh. "You've gone over your list at least a dozen times."

"I think I got a little carried away." Binky peered into a mixing bowl covered with a dish towel. "Maybe we should have ordered pizzas instead of trying to make them ourselves."

"It's a little late now," Jennifer said sarcastically. "The dough is rising and the ingredients are sitting on the counter."

"I want it to be so special. I think we should welcome Peggy home in the best possible way we can. Don't you?"

"Of course. And homemade pizza is her favorite."

Binky blushed and gave a shy smile. "Harry's, too."

That was part of the reason Binky was so rattled tonight. Harry Cramer was home for two days and had agreed to come to the party. Binky always acted a little giddy in Harry's presence.

"We'll have a do-it-yourself party," Lexi said. "Everything's going to be fine. Once everybody's hungry, we'll assign people jobs. Some will work on the pizza crust, others will be in charge of spreading the tomato sauce and cheese. Those who don't work on the pizza will get to build the sundaes."

"I think it sounds great," Jennifer enthused, sneaking another handful of shredded mozzarella.

"I don't think there's anything that can go wrong. . . ." Binky's voice trailed away. Her brother Egg poked his head around the kitchen door. "Oh-oh. Forget I said that."

"What's going on in here?" he asked. "The music's playing in the living room and everything's set up."

"There's nothing in here that should interest you, Egg," Binky said abruptly. "Scram. If you hang around, we'll give you a job."

Egg ignored her and entered the kitchen.

Lexi turned away to hide her smile. Binky and Egg were the funniest pair she'd ever known. They were utterly loyal to each other, but at the same time felt perfectly free to criticize each other without mercy. They were always getting into silly arguments. As usual, Egg couldn't keep his nose out of things and Binky couldn't keep her mouth shut about it.

"Are you sure you have enough pizza ingredients," he wondered, peeking under the dish towel. "This doesn't look like much crust dough."

"What do you know about it? You can't cook," Binky said indignantly.

"I bought six cans of chocolate syrup. Do you think that's going to be enough?"

"We're not planning to drink it. We're planning to serve it on ice cream."

Egg meandered around the kitchen examining things on the counters. "Ah-hah!" he pointed a long skinny finger toward a stack of paper napkins. "I knew I couldn't trust you. Look what you've done."

"What have we done?"

"You should be using cloth napkins," Egg said indignantly. "Cloth napkins are reusable. We've discussed that."

Oh-oh, Lexi thought to herself. Egg was wearing his environmental police hat again. That could mean trouble.

"We don't have enough cloth napkins for the entire group, Egg," Lexi pointed out gently. "But we do use them for our family every day. I think that counts, don't you?"

"I suppose," Egg mumbled. He was already down on his knees in front of the kitchen sink. He opened the door and peeked inside, reading the labels on all the cleaning products.

"Now what?" Binky shrugged her shoulders, as puzzled by her brother's behavior as Lexi was.

"Have you read the labels on these cans and bottles?" Egg asked. His voice was muffled as it floated up from the cabinet. "Half of them aren't biodegradable. Does your mother know about this?"

Binky let out a little squawk and grabbed a dishtowel. She began beating Egg over the back with it. "Get out of there. Get out of there!"

He scurried backward, away from the sink and stood up. "What are you doing?"

"You're driving me crazy. You can't go into other people's homes and criticize their paper products and examine things under their sinks."

"But this is Lexi's house. She understands. She's one of us."

Lexi controlled her giggles long enough to put her arm around Egg. "It's okay, Binky. I don't mind. I understand your brother."

"Well, that's more than I can say. He's so incredibly embarrassing. He expects me to think of the final impact of every single thing I do. If I did that, I'd have to hide in my room all day."

"Well, at least then you wouldn't be polluting the water or wasting it," Egg pointed out matter-of-factly.

Binky's pale gray-green eyes widened until Lexi thought they might pop right out of her head. "So that's what you think, Edward McNaughton. Why, I ought to . . ." Binky plucked a spatula from the counter top and approached Egg, waving it menacingly.

"Put that thing down, Binky. I'm sure Mr. and Mrs. Leighton don't approve of violence in their household."

"I'm sure they don't approve of *you* in their household either, crawling around in their cupboards and criticizing their purchases."

"Hey, Egg," Todd yelled from the back steps. "Come out here and turn the crank on this ice cream maker for a few minutes. Harry and I are getting tired."

Egg escaped and Binky laid down the spatula with a little growl. "That brother of mine."

"You're crazy about him and you know it," Lexi pointed out.

"I think maybe I'm just crazy." Binky gave a sheepish grin. "But I do like him."

"You'd never know it by the way you act around each other," Jennifer commented.

"That's half the fun of having a brother."

Lexi was accustomed to Binky and Egg's little spats. Binky and Egg were each other's own best friends . . . and worst enemies. The doorbell rang sharply, making all three girls jump.

"It's her. It's her," Binky said, excitedly. "Peggy's here."

Lexi moved toward the front door with Binky and Jennifer close on her heels. Peggy stood on the porch with a shy smile on her face.

"It is so good to see you," Binky squealed.

"You look wonderful," Jennifer yelped. Both girls hugged Peggy enthusiastically.

"I'd almost forgotten what a beautiful shade of red your hair is."

"I think you're a little taller."

"That's going to be great for the basketball team, isn't it?"

The girls kept up a running battery of comments.

Peggy remained silent, although smiling at her babbling friends.

She looked wonderful in a copper-colored jumpsuit with a wide belt. Her waist was slim and trim. No one would ever have guessed that she'd recently had a baby. That, apparently, was the way Peggy wanted it. At that moment, Egg, Todd and Harry trailed into the living room, wiping their hands on the legs of their jeans.

"Hey, Peggy," Egg yelped, then turned suddenly shy. "Good to have you back," he said softly.

Todd put his arm around Peggy and gave her a big hug. "You remember Harry Cramer, don't you?" Harry grinned.

"Well, don't just stand in the doorway. Come in." Jennifer pulled Peggy into the room. "Tell us everything we ever wanted to know about Arizona. Is it hot? Is it dry? Is it all desert? Do they have mountains?"

"What are the kids like? How was your school? How does it rate next to Cedar River?"

"Were you in any extracurricular activities? Did you play basketball?"

"Too bad the girls' team couldn't come tonight. They had a meeting."

"What's their school paper like? Did you write for it?" The questions went on and on. Peggy, laughing, allowed herself to be pulled into the room and surrounded by her friends.

Todd slipped his arm around Lexi's shoulders. She sat curled against him listening to Peggy's stories about traveling to Mexico. When Todd shifted on the couch, Lexi slid away. Did it bother Peggy to see her and Todd together like that? Did it remind her of Chad? Were they being rude?

Todd laughed at the story Peggy was telling. His dark eyes sparkled and his golden hair tossed carelessly across his forehead. *Dear, sweet Todd.* He was Lexi's dearest and best friend. He was kind, considerate, thoughtful, caring. But Lexi was sure Peggy would have said those very same things about Chad.

Lexi felt a little guilty that they hadn't invited Chad here tonight. Still, it didn't seem quite right since Peggy hadn't mentioned him.

Silently, Lexi vowed never to get into the kind of situation in which Peggy had found herself. No matter how much she might love Todd, she would never have sex with a man before marriage.

"It's build-your-own-pizza time," Binky announced. "Let's get started."

The entire group trooped into the kitchen. Egg, of course, took on the job of supervisor and managed to stick either his nose or his fingers into everyone else's business. When the pizzas were baked, they took them into the dining room and finished them off with great enthusiasm.

"I think I'm going to explode," Harry announced with a groan. "How much did I eat?"

"You ate an entire pizza," Binky pointed out cheerfully.

"It was great," Peggy said with a genuine smile. "I haven't had pizza that good since I left Cedar River."

"I think somebody's going to have to roll me home," Jennifer groaned. "I feel like a beach ball."

"You all look like a bunch of lizards sunning yourselves on the sidewalk," Todd observed as the group lounged around the Leighton living room.

"Oh, great. First my brother tells me I'd be better off staying in my room than polluting the country-side, and now Todd tells me I look like a lizard. Am I going to get a complex or what?" Binky asked.

"Speaking of complexes," Peggy said, "how is Minda?" Everyone laughed.

"Same as ever. She still thinks she's the best thing around since sliced bread."

"And the Hi-Fives?"

"The same. They still go around ignoring mere mortals like us," Binky sighed.

"Matt Windsor's doing okay," Jennifer inter-jected with a smile. "He's going away for the summer. You'll have to wait until school starts in the fall to see him."

When the news from Cedar River High School was exhausted Egg made an announcement. "I've in-vented a new game. Would everyone like to try it?"

"What kind of a game?" Todd asked cautiously.

"A question and answer game. You'll like it. I call it 'trash trivia'."

"You're kidding, right? This is a joke."

"Who'd ever think of anything as dumb as that?"

"Egg? You *are* kidding, aren't you?"

"Oh, leave him alone, you guys," Peggy said. "If Egg has a game, I think we should try it."

"Peggy, you don't know what you're getting your-self into," Binky warned. "My brother has trash on his brain." She giggled. "I didn't mean that quite the way it sounded."

Egg whipped a stack of note cards out of his hip

pocket. "This is how 'trash trivia' works. I'll ask you a question about the environment, pollution or some related subject. If you get the answer right, you get a point. If you get it wrong, your points are taken away. Here's a question." Egg plucked a note card from the stack. "Name three things you can do to conserve energy."

"Sleep more! Eat more! Work less!"

"I'm not kidding you guys. Here are the answers: Drive your car less; turn off lights when you're not using them; turn down the furnace in winter and the air conditioner in summer."

"I like my ideas better," Harry said teasingly.

"Give me another 'trash trivia' question," Peggy said.

"What's one way to save on gasoline?"

"Don't drive," Harry hooted.

Egg gave him a dirty look. "You inflate the tires properly. Tires will not wear out as quickly and your car will use less gas."

Harry blinked. He was surprised and interested. "I didn't realize that. What else have you got in those 'trash trivia' cards?"

"How many years does it take for disposable diapers to decompose?"

Now the whole group was getting into Egg's game.

"Five years."

"Ten years."

"A hundred years."

Egg kept shaking his head. "It takes five hundred years for disposable diapers to decompose in a landfill."

"Five hundred years," Binky made an awful face. "You're kidding. That's the most disgusting thing I've ever heard."

"The truth," Egg said confidently. "That's why we should be telling everyone we know with babies that they should be using cloth diapers. And do you know that those styrofoam cups we use are completely non-biodegradable? That means they won't *ever* decompose."

"Ever? Ever, never, ever?" Binky wondered.

"That's right."

"Ooooh." Binky made a face. "Who wants to live on a planet with stacks of styrofoam cups lying around!"

"My point exactly."

They'd played almost an hour when Harry announced, "Hey, Egg, this game isn't half bad. In fact, it's fun."

Egg grinned. "You don't mind if I say 'I told you so', do you?"

"I don't know how I can stop you."

Everyone was eating ice cream sundaes when Egg excused himself and disappeared toward the back of the house. Fifteen minutes later, Binky looked around the room. "Where's my brother? He's been gone for a long time. Do you think something is wrong?"

Todd stood up. "I'll check on him."

"I'll go too," Harry said. "I hope he isn't sick."

"If he is, it's all that pizza he ate," Binky said unsympathetically.

Moments later, a roar of laughter came from the Leighton bathroom. When Egg, Todd and Harry returned, Egg's face was bright red. Todd and Harry were breathless with laughter.

"What's going on, you guys?" Lexi asked.

"Guess what we found Egg doing?" Harry said.

"I can't imagine."

"He had the lid off the back of the toilet, Lexi. Did you know that this guy was carrying a brick in his jacket pocket?"

Lexi stared at Egg, dumbfounded.

"Don't look at me like that," Egg said. "Do you realize how much water you can save by displacing the water in the toilet tank with a brick?"

"Don't you think my dad should take care of that sort of thing?"

Egg's ears got pink. "I suppose, but I thought if I just carried a brick or two around and just slipped it in the bathroom without anyone knowing . . ."

"I can see it all now," Todd said as if reading an imaginary banner, "Edward 'Egg' McNaughton for President. His campaign promise: a brick in every toilet, a smile on every face."

Peggy burst out laughing. She laughed until she cried.

Egg's face was as red as the tomato sauce on the leftover pizza.

"You know," Peggy said with a chuckle, "I think Egg might be right."

"You do?" Egg said hopefully, his eyes brightening.

"It sounds really funny when you put it your way, but in Arizona, there are lots of environmental campaigns going on. My cousin took part in one. She helped publish an environmental newsletter, printed on recycled paper. It was put out by an all-volunteer group, and distributed to grocery stores and service stations all over the state. They really got the message out about taking care of the environment."

"You know, I like that idea," Todd said. "Maybe we could do something like that."

"I'm sure the grocery stores wouldn't mind if we put flyers out," Binky agreed.

"My pastor's been doing a lot of talking lately about being good stewards of God's gifts. Maybe he'd let us talk about it in church one day," Lexi suggested. "This is the perfect opportunity to be a good steward and to tell people about making the best of the gifts God's given them."

"We have all the talent we need." Egg was getting excited. "Lexi, Todd and I are already on the staff of the *Cedar River Review*. You guys can be the investigative reporters while the three of us put together a brochure."

Eagerly they gathered around the dining room table to plan their new project.

Jennifer spoke up. "I can find a source of recycled paper. My dad will help me."

"Great." Lexi began recording a list of assignments. "Jennifer is in charge of the paper. Binky, what do you want to do?"

"I could find somebody to print it."

"My dad has a computer. He might let us do some desk-top publishing."

"I'll be in charge of lay-out," Egg offered. "That's what I do for the *Review*."

"And Lexi and I will do the photos, the headlines and the editing," Todd volunteered. "It will be easy after putting together the school paper."

"I wish I were going to be here so I could help you out," Harry said regretfully. "If you want me to, I can spread the newsletter around school."

"Sounds good to me," Todd said with a nod.

"It's settled then? Are we all going to be environmental reporters?" Todd asked. He glanced at Egg who was grinning widely.

"What's so funny, McNaughton?" Todd said suspiciously.

Egg's grin nearly cracked his face. "If you hadn't caught me fooling with the Leightons' toilet, none of this would have happened. And you were *laughing* at me."

"Egg, you'll have to face up to the fact that anytime you stick your head in the back of someone's toilet, I'm going to laugh."

Enthusiasm was running high as the party guests began to leave.

Peggy was the last to go. "Thanks, Lexi, for everything. I really appreciated this opportunity to break the ice. I thought it would be hard to come back to my friends. I see now that they're what I missed most of all."

"We're here for you anytime, remember that."

"This newspaper thing might be good for me. It'll give me something to think about other than the baby. There are days when I simply can't get her out of my mind. Maybe this little newsletter will be a distraction."

Lexi moved around the living room picking up dirty dishes and turning out lights. She'd learned something from Peggy's experience. One bad decision could affect a lifetime.

Chapter Ten

Lexi awoke to the sound of the garbage truck, roaring and grinding in the alley behind her house. She'd never even noticed what time of day garbage pick-up was scheduled until Egg started his environmental campaign. Now, as she lay with her eyes half-open and the sun streaming across her face, she began to think about—of all the crazy things—the trash.

With her mother's help, they'd put five plastic bins in the kitchen closet—one for paper, one for cardboard and one each for plastic, aluminum and glass. They'd also made spaces for stacks of newspapers and another for junk mail that had been printed on one side only. Ben loved to have a ready supply of drawing paper. It amazed everyone how much paper actually went through the household in a week. The trash-sorting system had become something of a game for the entire family.

Lexi had begun to dislike the little plastic bubbles that Ben's toys often came packaged in. They were not recyclable. Neither was the plastic wrap that she'd freely used to cover leftovers. Her mother had begun using glass jars and glass-covered dishes for storing them.

111

The grinding gears and squawk of unoiled hinges outside her window reminded Lexi of the whole new concept that had come into her life. It was odd how one's ideas could change in such a short time. Lexi had never given garbage a second thought before. She'd assumed, like most people, that when the sanitation department picked up the refuse, it was carried off to a place where it magically disappeared, never to be seen again.

Now, Lexi knew that all garbage went to a landfill to be buried. Though much of the refuse there would disintegrate over the years, some remained intact. Archaeologists digging up a landfill hundreds of years from now would discover that this generation was careless, wasteful, and extravagant. They would uncover the mass of disposable diapers and indestructible plastic and styrofoam packaging that would stay on the earth forever.

There was no point in trying to go back to sleep now. Lexi could hear her mother and father moving around in the kitchen. With a yawn and stretch, she rolled to the side of the bed. She slipped into a pair of shorts and an over-sized T-shirt with the logo "Save the Trees" that Egg had given her and padded downstairs barefoot.

Her parents were drinking their morning coffee and watching the action at the bird feeder outside the kitchen window.

"Good morning, Lexi," Dr. Leighton said. "Did you have a good rest?"

"Until the garbage truck came. I didn't realize how noisy it was."

"You mean you've always slept through that roar until now?"

"I think Lexi's becoming aware of some of the more unglamorous aspects of life, Jim." Mrs. Leighton set a bowl of oatmeal in front of Lexi.

"I've noticed a new consciousness when we go shopping," Mrs. Leighton continued, winking at Lexi. "We have to read every single label. I can only buy detergents and soaps that are concentrated to last a long time and come in biodegradable, or recyclable containers. Besides that, Lexi wouldn't let me buy a paring knife the other day because it was packaged in a plastic bubble."

Mr. Leighton took another sip of his steaming coffee. "Saving the earth is a good thing to be enthused about, Lexi. I'm proud of you."

"Sometimes I don't feel like it's helping much," Lexi admitted. "It seems like all that my friends and I are talking about lately is garbage."

Mr. Leighton threw back his head and laughed. "It isn't very pleasant, is it? But think of what you're working for. Uncut forests. Fewer landfills. Clean water. Clean air. God's green earth. Those are pretty wonderful things to think about, Lexi.

"In the adult forum in Sunday school, we discussed this very topic. You should be proud of yourselves. You're making adults see that stewardship is much more than a gift of money. It's a gift of time and effort."

"Thanks, Dad. I needed a pep talk this morning," Lexi said. "Last night I dreamed that I was drowning in polluted water, with dead fish and candy wrappers floating all around me."

"Sounds like you need a change of pace, Lexi. What are your plans for the day?" Mrs. Leighton poured herself another cup of coffee.

"First of all, I thought I'd go to the nursing home and say hello to Grandma Carson. I haven't seen her for a while."

"Why don't you go now, dear? She seems to be less confused in the morning."

After breakfast, Lexi rode her bike to the nursing home. Parking it in a bike rack out front, she headed slowly toward the main doors of the home. It was always difficult to see her grandmother because it was impossible to predict whether she would recognize Lexi or call her by some other name.

"Good morning, Lexi," said the nurse at the station with a smile. "How are you today? Your grandmother has just finished breakfast; I'm sure she'll be glad for company."

"I hope so." Lexi paused for a moment before the door to her grandmother's room. "Please, God, help me with this."

Grandmother was sitting in a rocking chair staring at two love birds in a cage near her bed. At the sound of Lexi's footsteps, she looked up.

"Hello there. And who are you, my dear?" Grandma asked sweetly.

"Lexi, your granddaughter. Do you remember me, Grandma?"

Mrs. Carson brushed her fingers across her forehead. "Lexi. Yes, I remember her. Hello, dear. How are you?"

Lexi breathed a little sigh of relief. The birds in the cage twittered and chirped.

"Aren't they lovely?" Grandmother stared at the birds fondly. "I could sit and watch them all day."

Lexi knew there were days when that's exactly what her grandmother did—watched the little birds fluttering in their cage.

"Mom and Dad said to say 'hi,' Grandma."

Grandmother Carson's face became a mask of confusion. "Mom and Dad. Now who are they?"

"Jim and Marilyn Leighton." Lexi knew that her grandmother's mind couldn't hold on to memories of people or places once so familiar.

"Oh, Jim and Marilyn," Grandmother's face creased into a smile. "They're very nice people, aren't they?"

After the few moments of ordinary exchanges Grandmother Carson was already tired.

"I'm going to leave now, Grandmother," Lexi said softly. She patted her grandmother's gnarled hand. "I think you'd like to watch the birds for a while."

"Aren't they pretty? I love the birds," Grandma said, her eyes focused on the little gold cage. Quietly, Lexi tiptoed from the room.

"Hello, Lexi." The director of the rest home, Mr. Franklin, greeted her in the hallway. "How is your grandmother doing?"

"About the same. Happy, but very confused. She wasn't sure who my parents were today."

"Alzheimer's is a strange disease, Lexi. There's no way to recapture the wonderful mind that is lost. It's heartbreaking."

Lexi's own heart felt the pain of the debilitating disease that had taken her grandmother's mind.

"Sorry I can't shake your hand, Lexi," Mr. Franklin said. "I've been digging in the dirt."

"Oh, doing some gardening?" Lexi asked.

"Actually, I was planting trees. I'm involved in a city tree-planting project. It's an off-shoot of the 'Clean Up Cedar River' effort. We've decided to plant several trees around the city. They reduce pollution because they assist in oxygen production."

"I think that's a great idea! My friends and I have started our own environmental campaign."

"You have? I'm glad to see teenagers getting involved in this issue. It's important to all of us. You young people will inherit the earth that we're using today. I'd like to give it to you in good shape," he said with a broad smile.

"Would you have time for an interview, Mr. Franklin?"

"An interview?"

Lexi explained about the newsletter that she and her friends were going to produce.

"Why, I think that's a wonderful idea. I'd be honored to be interviewed for your brochure, Lexi. And, by the way, when it's ready, you can bring some here to the home; I can distribute them to the guests of our residents. I do have a few moments right now. Would you like to do the interview here?"

Lexi agreed enthusiastically, and Mr. Franklin got some paper and a pen for her from the reception desk.

Soon they were deep in discussion about the importance trees played in the atmosphere and in the environment.

The interview was winding down when Lexi said, "Instead of just planting these trees in your spare time, maybe your group should declare a formal tree-planting day in Cedar River and ask every family to plant at least one tree. Some businesses or organizations might be willing to donate funds for trees. Children could be commissioned to water and care for the trees in public places."

Mr. Franklin nodded his approval. "I think that's a wonderful idea. I don't see why we couldn't go all out with this thing. We could have a band. Speakers. Make the entire city aware of our environmental problem, instead of just a small group of concerned citizens. I'm going to look into it this afternoon."

"Well, sir, if there's anything we can do to help . . ."

"If this comes to pass, we're going to need lots of publicity, Lexi. Maybe that newsletter you're working on can help us out."

"We'll do *all* the publicity if you want us to."

"I'll keep that in mind. You're a very admirable young woman, Miss Leighton. I've watched the care and concern you show for your grandmother and I'm impressed with the interest you have in our city. I'm very happy to know you, Lexi."

Her head was spinning by the time she left the nursing home. She felt honored by the compliments Mr. Franklin had paid her. What was more exciting was the possibility of letting others know about the concerns of preserving the environment. There was so much to be said about saving energy and water, avoiding toxins and pollutants, reducing waste and recycling. Lexi smiled to herself. She could get as enthused and silly about this whole thing as Egg if she weren't careful.

Swinging her leg over the seat of her bike, she pushed off, eager to talk to Todd. She found him changing the oil in one of the cars in his brother Mike's shop. He was greasy and grimy as usual, but looked wonderful to Lexi.

"What's up, Lexi?" Todd looked up.

The story of her interview with the nursing home director and the "Cedar River Tree-planting Day" idea bubbled out. As Todd listened, his handsome face broke into a wide smile. "Lexi, I think that's great. Not only will it give us something to write about in our newsletter, but we'll get some terrific publicity as well." He kicked at the tire of the car he had been working on. "In fact, I'd like to do an article about driving more energy-efficient cars. I want to tell people how important it is to use radial tires, obey the speed laws and have regular tune-ups. Of course, using public transportation, car pools or your legs saves even more energy."

"Do it," Lexi said. "Write the article."

"Wait until Egg hears this. He'll be proud of us."

Lexi looked at her watch. "I'm supposed to answer phones at my dad's office this afternoon. Maybe I can get my article typed there."

Leaving the garage, Lexi went directly to her father's veterinary office. Her dad met her at the front door.

"Hello, Lexi. You've come early. I'm glad. My secretary had to go to the post office. The phone has been ringing like crazy. Can you start work right away? I suppose you haven't had lunch yet, but we can call something in. This is going to be a very busy day." Just then, the telephone rang.

"Get that, will you Lexi? I have to get back to work."

"Hello, Leighton Veterinary Clinic. Reuse. Recycle. Restore," she added impulsively.

Lexi was swept into the afternoon's work. There wasn't a spare moment for the newsletter article or anything else, other than the jobs her father had waiting for her. Not even Peggy Madison and her troubles entered Lexi's mind.

Chapter Eleven

"Are you going to bed soon, Lexi?" Mrs. Leighton asked. "Ben's already sound asleep."

It had been a busy day, but Lexi was still excited about the progress that was being made for the Cedar River Day celebration. The first draft of the newsletter was coming along nicely. Lexi needed to be quiet and gather her thoughts. "I'll go out on the porch for a while, if that's all right."

"Be sure to lock the door and turn off the lights when you come to bed. Goodnight, darling." Mrs. Leighton kissed her daughter lightly on the top of her head. "Lexi, by the way, have you seen Peggy Madison lately?"

"I've talked to her on the phone a couple times, but she's seldom home when I call."

"I was just wondering if you girls were having any problems."

"No. No problems, Mom."

Lexi opened the front door and slipped onto the porch. She settled herself in a large wicker rocker and stared out at the street. *At least there are no problems on my end,* she thought. Still, it was odd that she'd seen and heard so little of Peggy. Was something wrong with her friend?

Lexi had been on the porch only fifteen minutes, jotting notes to herself about the newsletter, when she heard footsteps along the sidewalk. She peered into the darkness. "Hello? Who's there?"

"Lexi? Are you alone?"

"Hi, Peggy," Lexi said, recognizing her friend's voice. "Everyone's in bed. Come on up."

Peggy stepped into the dim glow of the porch light.

Something *was* wrong. "What is it?" Lexi reached for her friend's hand. Peggy drew a ragged, sobbing breath, and Lexi led her to a chair. "Sit down. Tell me what's wrong."

Her eyes puffy, and her cheeks tear-stained, Peggy began to cry. Mascara ran down her face in little streaks.

Lexi instinctively reached for a box of tissue, and then began to rub Peggy's back and whisper, "It's all right, Peggy. Calm down."

Nothing seemed to help. Finally, Lexi ran into the house and poured a glass of cold water. When she gave it to her, Peggy's shoulders were trembling, but the sobbing had ceased.

Lexi had also brought a damp cloth from the kitchen, and began to wipe the tears from her friend's face.

Peggy's usually neat hair was disheveled and her clothes were wrinkled.

"Want to talk about it?" Lexi asked softly.

Peggy's voice was thin and raspy. "I went out with Chad tonight. I'd been putting off seeing him, as you know. There's been so much we needed to discuss, and I thought we should just do it and get it over with."

Lexi nodded and waited for her friend to continue.

"It was more uncomfortable than I imagined it would be. It's difficult to make conversation after you've gone away, had a child, and given it up for adoption. The baby was ours—together. It's so hard to explain the feelings, Lexi."

Lexi couldn't even begin to imagine how it would feel.

"I let him hold my hand," Peggy's voice was resigned. "I thought it was the least I could do. After we talked for a while, we went to the Hamburger Shack for a soda."

"Sounds normal. What's made you so upset, Peggy?"

"Well, after we left the Hamburger Shack, I thought Chad would take me home. We still hadn't really resolved anything—about us, about the future, about the baby. Instead, he drove his car to our old parking spot and turned off the engine."

"And you talked there?"

"Talked?" Peggy laughed bitterly. "That was the *last* thing Chad had on his mind. He wanted to pick up where we'd left off, Lexi. I guess he assumed I'd done something to prevent becoming pregnant again."

Lexi felt sick to her stomach. "You're kidding."

"I wouldn't joke about a thing like this, Lexi. All he was interested in was getting me into the back seat of the car. He didn't seem to care how I felt or what I had to say. He didn't want to hear any more about Arizona or how my life had changed. The only person Chad was interested in was himself."

"What did you do?"

"I talked." Peggy's eyes filled with tears again. "I talked until I my throat was raw, but I couldn't make him understand. He didn't want to listen, Lexi. He didn't want to admit that what we'd done was wrong. He didn't even want to think about the fact that we'd had a baby. It's crazy, isn't it? What's happened in the last nine months has changed my life completely and doesn't seem to have touched Chad's one little bit."

"I can't believe it!" Lexi exclaimed. "While you were gone, Chad was very quiet, kept to himself. I guess I assumed he was thinking about you and . . . the baby."

"He was, Lexi. He thought about it all winter. And he came to the conclusion that he wanted to just ignore the past. He told me that. 'Just forget it,' he said, 'You're making a mountain out of a molehill.' He said that I was dumb not to have looked into some kind of birth control in all this time, because I knew that he'd be waiting for me at home. He said that the baby was gone and that we should get on with our lives."

Lexi had had no idea how cold, calculating and heartless Chad Allen could be.

Peggy was quivering like a leaf. "And then he tried to force himself on me."

"What?"

"I thought I knew Chad. I thought I loved him." Peggy shook her head. "I was so wrong about him."

"Did he hurt you, Peggy?"

"He twisted my arm, and tore my skirt. He accused me of teasing him, leading him on. He said I'd already lost my virginity and there was no way I could get that back."

"How awful! How could he be so insensitive after all you've been through?"

"I don't know, Lexi. He just doesn't understand. He never saw our baby. It's all so unreal to him." Her voice broke. "What am I going to do, Lexi? I'm lucky I could break away from him and come here without him following me."

"First of all, you should never see Chad again."

"I suppose not. I wish I could make him understand how I felt, what I went through, how terrified I was."

"Why is that so difficult for him?" Lexi asked.

"He never even saw me pregnant. When I left here, I wasn't even showing, of course. Now, I've come back the same as I was—at least outwardly. It probably doesn't seem possible to him that he's fathered a child. I didn't tell him at the time what I was feeling and thinking because it hurt too much. He doesn't know what an ordeal it was."

"Well, you can't make excuses for him, Peggy. Nothing gives him the right to treat you the way he has."

"No, I guess not. But . . ."

"Have you ever heard of 'date rape,' Peggy?"

"Yes, I guess so."

"Don't you see? Isn't that what nearly happened tonight? Chad was trying to force you into something that you didn't want. If he had succeeded, it would have been rape."

"Aren't people usually raped by strangers?"

"No one—friend or stranger—should force some-one into something they don't want to do. No one has that right. It doesn't matter that you and Chad were very close before. If you've decided that the relation-ship should change or end, then he doesn't have the right to force you." Lexi felt like her blood would boil. "Chad can't love you and be violent toward you, Peggy. You shouldn't see him anymore."

Peggy looked uncertain. "So, you think we should break up?"

"Don't you *want* to break up?"

"Yes, but . . ."

What was wrong with Peggy? Lexi wondered. If she wanted to break up with Chad, why didn't she just do it? Why was she so . . . fearful?

Lexi touched Peggy's arm. "Are you afraid of Chad for some reason?"

"I never was . . . until tonight."

"Because he tried to force himself on you?"

"Partly."

"What else?"

"Chad was so intense tonight."

"Intense?" Lexi questioned. "I don't understand."

"So serious. So determined. So strong." Peggy tried to explain. "Once before, a long time ago, I men-tioned breaking up with Chad, so that we could date other people for a while."

"Oh? What did he say?" Lexi didn't remember Peggy mentioning this before.

"Chad got so upset that it really frightened me. I didn't dare bring up the subject again. He worried and fretted about it for days. He didn't want to stop talking about it. He'd call me at night and tell me how much he cared for me, that it would break his heart if we ever split up." Peggy shivered. "He really scared me, Lexi."

"How?"

"I thought he might hurt himself—or me."

This was a side of Chad Allen that Lexi had never seen before. It angered and terrified her at the same time. "Peggy, you've got to stand up for yourself. You can't let Chad push you around. If Chad is going to hurt you, stay away from him. Chad does not own you. He can't control your life. You are in charge of your life . . . God is in charge of your life. What Chad chooses to do is Chad's problem, not yours."

"My parents don't want me to go out with Chad anymore . . . and I've certainly prayed, asking God what I should do."

"Then you've talked to all the right people," Lexi said. "Your earthly parents and your heavenly one. Think about what's best for *you* in this instance, Peggy. Chad's thinking about what's best for himself."

"I really appreciate your concern for me, Lexi."

"Well, it makes me so furious to think that Chad would try to force himself on you!"

Lexi sensed that Peggy was feeling guilty too. Guilty about giving up the baby. Guilty about hurting Chad. Guilty about disappointing her parents. But God had forgiven Peggy—now Peggy had to forgive herself.

"Listen, Peggy, you're one of my dearest friends in the whole world." Lexi rested her hand on Peggy's arm. "Do what you know is right. You're smart. Don't let yourself be manipulated."

"Chad scares me. He makes . . . threats."

"Threats? What kind of threats?"

"I don't want to talk about it, really. It's too awful."

"Peggy, what kind of threats has Chad made?" Lexi felt as if she were looking into Peggy's soul through her eyes.

"Sometimes he says he'll kill himself if he ever has to live without me."

"He told you that?"

"Yes."

"Peggy, you can't let Chad manipulate you like this. Do *you* want to continue your relationship with him?"

"No. Not when he expects me to continue to be intimate with him. I've made up my mind that I will not become involved like that with anyone again— not until I'm married. I made one mistake. I won't make it again. I want to start over, Lexi. The way I was . . . before the baby."

"Talk to your parents, Peggy. Tell them what's going on."

"But it would hurt them."

"Hurt them? Peggy, they've already been hurt. Can you imagine what a mistake it would have been if you hadn't confided in them about your pregnancy?"

"You're right. And they were great. Very supportive. I couldn't have gotten through it without them."

"Of course not," Lexi said, encouraging her friend. "They stood by you through your pregnancy. They'll be glad to know you want to recapture some of what you've lost. And they'll certainly want to know if someone is mistreating their daughter."

"Oh, Lexi, I'm so confused. Sometimes I wish I could die."

Lexi held Peggy's hands tightly. "Talk to your parents. Confide in them. Tell them everything you've told me—about Chad, about your feelings, about how confused you are. Don't keep it inside, Peggy. This is much too important. *You're* too important."

"But I don't know what they'll think."

"I'm sure they won't be shocked. They'll probably even expect it. You've been through an awful experience."

"I don't know. I just don't know."

"Will you let me pray with you, Peggy?"

Peggy nodded, trying to hold back the tears.

"Dear Father," Lexi began, "we're scared. We don't know what to do. Peggy's in a bad situation right now. She needs your help and your guidance. She doesn't want to go out with Chad anymore. But he's being unreasonable. He's threatening her to get his way. Help Peggy to know what to do and how to answer Chad. And make Peggy's parents really wise so they can give her the right sort of advice. And Father, show Chad that what he's doing is wrong. Lord, I pray for everyone in this situation. Please put your healing hand on every heart and mind. I pray this in Jesus' name. Amen."

"Amen," Peggy echoed. Her expression was one of surprise. "You talk to God like that? About ordinary things and feelings?"

"I talk to God about everything, just like I talk to you. I probably talk to Him twenty times a day—

about things that I want to thank Him for or that I want His opinion on. God and I have lots of conversations, Peggy. You should try it."

"I do pray."

"Maybe you're too formal in your prayers. I keep a running dialogue going with God about what's happening all day long." Lexi grinned knowingly. "There's no better conversation to have than one with God. He always listens."

The girls sat on the steps and continued to talk quietly about whatever came to their minds. A certain peace came over them. Peggy began to yawn and rub her eyes. "I think I'd better go home now. Thanks, Lexi—for everything."

"Are you feeling better, Peggy?"

"I think so. I know that I have two things to do when I get home."

"What's that?" Lexi asked.

"I have a couple of conversations I want to start. One with my parents, and the other with God."

Chapter Twelve

Lexi hadn't been able to concentrate all day. Her mind and hands just weren't working together. Each time she thought of Peggy and her experience with Chad, she began to tremble.

Date rape wasn't a foreign concept to Lexi. She'd read about it in magazines. She and her mother had had a frank talk about the expectations boys sometimes have of girls. But it was an issue that hadn't seemed real until now.

Lexi was listlessly watering plants outside when Peggy arrived. She swung off her bike and punched the kickstand into place. "Lexi!"

The hose clattered to the ground, water splattering through the dirt. "Peggy, are you all right?"

Peggy's cheeks were flushed, her eyes wet. But she didn't look as upset as she had the night before.

"I have something to tell you."

Lexi glanced around. Ben and a playmate were meandering through the yard pretending they were a train.

"Come up to my room," Lexi offered. "We can be alone there."

Silently, the two of them made their way up the

stairs. Peggy sank onto the bed exhausted.

"I broke up with Chad."

"This morning?"

Peggy nodded. "I hardly slept at all last night thinking about what happened between us. No one can treat me that way, Lexi. No one. I understand that Chad is upset and not thinking clearly, but he can't force me to do anything. I thought he loved me, Lexi. I see now that his definition of love and mine are entirely different."

"What did Chad say?" Lexi was curious. She admired Peggy's newly confident attitude.

Peggy's eyes revealed her pain. "He was terribly upset. He didn't want to break up. He promised me nothing like last night would ever happen again." Peggy's down-turned eyes and soft voice hinted at her despair. "But I can't believe him, Lexi. I don't trust him anymore."

"Did he accept your decision?"

"He didn't accept it at all. He denied it completely. He said eventually I'd come to my senses and change my mind. He promised to be waiting for me when that happened." Peggy's voice trembled. "I told him it would never happen. I told him that it was over between us."

"And?"

"Chad said that if I didn't come back to him, he'd kill himself."

The hairbrush in Lexi's hand clattered to the floor. "What? He really told you that again?"

"He told me he'd wait until I changed my mind. If I didn't, he would kill himself."

"Oh, Peggy, no."

"I feel like I'm being blackmailed, Lexi. I can't understand why he's doing this to me."

"Do you think he was serious?"

"He was serious all right."

"What did you do?" Lexi's heart was in her throat.

"I didn't give in to his threats, Lexi. I couldn't. Not after the other night when he intentionally tried to hurt me."

"Then what did he do?"

"He told me that if I thought I felt badly about the baby, it was nothing compared to what I was going to feel when he died."

Lexi shuddered and reached for the top of her dresser to steady herself.

"I won't be manipulated anymore, Lexi. I won't. I can't. Not even if he threatens to kill himself. I just can't do it." Peggy began to weep with loud, heart-wrenching sobs. "I don't know where he is, Lexi. He went off in a terrible huff. We screamed at each other and said horrible things to one another. It shouldn't be like this, Lexi. There was a time when Chad and I loved each other. I know we did."

Lexi felt like she was in water over her head. What could she say? What could she do?

"Maybe he's going to kill himself right now. I don't know. Or maybe it was all just a ploy to get me to change my mind. I can't tell. I don't know Chad anymore." Peggy's voice pitched to a wail. "I've ruined everything. I've done it all wrong. I hate myself. Maybe I'm the one who should . . ."

"Stop it!" Lexi's voice was sharp. "Don't say things like that. It's wrong. God doesn't want His children to hurt themselves or take their own lives.

It's wrong, Peggy, do you hear me? Wrong." Lexi was almost shouting now. Somehow, she had to get through to her friend who was so eaten with guilt.

There was a knock on the door. "Are you girls okay?" Mrs. Leighton's soft voice came through the door. "I thought I heard someone crying." The door opened slowly, and Mrs. Leighton stepped into the room. Lexi was still leaning against the dresser trembling and pale. Peggy was sitting on the bed, sobbing.

"I think you girls had better tell me what's going on," Mrs. Leighton said firmly. She moved toward Peggy and slipped her arm around the girl's shoulders. "I know you've had a tough time, Peggy. I know that life isn't easy for you right now. But I want you to know that you can talk about it. Here. Now."

Mrs. Leighton brushed a stray lock of hair out of Peggy's eyes. "Your mother confided in me about your pregnancy, Peggy. I know about the baby and I know why you went to Arizona. There's nothing that you can say to me that will surprise me, shock me or make me love you less than I do at this moment. I just want you to know that."

Those were the words Peggy needed to hear. Suddenly, like a broken dam, the story of Chad poured out. His demands. The attempted rape. The way he wanted to pick up where they'd left off. The choice he'd made to ignore the fact that they'd had a child together. When Peggy told her about Chad's threats to commit suicide, Mrs. Leighton's lips tightened grimly.

"I think Chad needs help as much as you do, Peggy, but it's not your responsibility to find it for him. Let me talk to your mother. Let us handle this. This is a problem for adults. Chad needs to talk to a counselor. Perhaps we've made a mistake by ignoring his part in all of this. It's common in teenage pregnancies. Because it's the girl who carries the child, whose body is changing, whose life is being turned upside down, sometimes we forget that there's a young man involved too."

"Do you think you could help him, Mrs. Leighton?" Peggy said, her face tear-streaked.

"I'm sure we can. We'll make every effort to talk to his parents and let them know Chad has some things to work through. Don't worry about this, Peggy. You don't need one more thing to worry about right now."

"Thank you." Peggy breathed a raspy sigh of relief. "You don't know how wonderful that sounds to me. It's been such a heavy burden these last months. I feel that I've carried it all alone." Her face twisted with pain. "But I deserved it, didn't I?"

Mrs. Leighton was startled. "Deserved it?"

"The pain. All the hurt. I deserved it all."

"Why do you say that, Peggy?"

"Because I got pregnant. I had no business having sex with Chad. I got swept up in the moment and brought a baby into this world that won't ever know its parents. I've hurt my own parents. Now Chad is threatening to kill himself." When Peggy spoke, the agony of her heart was evident. "I feel so *guilty*."

"It's over and done with now, Peggy. It's time to get on with your life."

"But how do I do that?" Peggy wondered. "Maybe I should just get back together with Chad. Then he wouldn't be angry and make threats." She laughed bitterly. "I feel guilty if I stay with him and I feel guilty if I don't. There's no way out, is there?"

"Two wrongs never make a right, Peggy. Getting back together with Chad isn't going to make everything right again."

"There's nothing that makes what I've done right."

Lexi's heart ached for her friend. She'd never seen anyone so consumed with guilt.

"I was too young to have sex. I was unmarried. I was foolish. I gave in to Chad's pressure." Peggy sobbed and talked at the same time, the words spilling out. "Every day I think about the baby and feel so much guilt. A mother should be able to take care of her own baby, Mrs. Leighton."

"You're needing some care yourself right now," Mrs. Leighton said softly.

Peggy didn't disagree. Instead, she nodded and curled into the comfort of Mrs. Leighton's embrace. She gently cradled the girl, rocking her back and forth, soothing away the pain and grief.

"You're too hard on yourself, Peggy," Mrs. Leighton said finally. "In Isaiah 64, verse 6, it says: 'All of us have become like one who is unclean, and all our righteous acts are like filthy rags; we all shrivel up like a leaf, and like the wind our sins sweep us away.' That verse reminds us that we're all sinful."

"Then how can God stand to look at us?" Peggy asked.

"Because He loves us. He created every one of us. And we're His. He loves us, but hates our sin. He doesn't hate *us*—only the sin within us."

Mrs. Leighton reached for the Bible on Lexi's bedside stand. "There's a passage in Peter that I'd like to read too." With practiced fingers, Mrs. Leighton found the page, 1 Peter 2:23–25. "Listen to this, Peggy:

> When they hurled their insults at him, he did not retaliate; when he suffered, he made no threats. Instead, he entrusted himself to him who judges justly. He himself bore our sins in his body on the tree, so that we might die to sins and live for righteousness; by his wounds you have been healed. For you were like sheep going astray, but now you have returned to the Shepherd and Overseer of your souls.

"Don't you see, Peggy? Christ took care of your sins. He bore them so you wouldn't have to. He offers you healing from all the things that have been wrong in your life. He offers guidance and wholeness. You don't have to feel guilty anymore, Peggy. Your sins are forgiven by the Greatest Power in the universe. You just have to ask Him to forgive you.

"Surely you know John 3:16: 'For God so loved the world that he gave his one and only Son, that whoever believes in him shall not perish but have eternal life.' "

Peggy nodded.

"The verses that follow aren't as familiar, but say something equally wonderful." Mrs. Leighton continued: " 'For God did not send his Son into the world to condemn the world, but to save the world through him. Whoever believes in him is not condemned, but whoever does not believe stands condemned already because he has not believed in the name of God's one and only Son.'

"If you accept Christ and His love, you're no longer guilty of anything. It's all washed away. Gone. Vanished."

"I . . . I . . . I just don't know anymore, Mrs. Leighton. I'm so confused. I thought I believed in God. I really did. I thought that I'd accepted Him as my personal Savior. But now, there's this thing with Chad. I'm just carrying this load of . . ."

"Guilt," Mrs. Leighton finished for her. "God wants to take away the guilt, Peggy."

"But how can He? How can I . . ."

"First John 1:9 says: 'If we confess our sins, he is faithful and just and will forgive us our sins and purify us from all unrighteousness.' God will make us clean from all the wrongs we have done."

"Just like that?" Peggy said doubtfully. "Isn't that too . . . easy?"

Mrs. Leighton smiled. "Easy, Peggy? Jesus died on a cross for us. There's nothing easy about that."

"All I have to do is believe?"

"Yes. Believe He died for you. Believe that if there were no other person on earth, Christ would still have died for Peggy Madison."

"If I were the only person on earth?"

"Absolutely," Mrs. Leighton said confidently. "That's what's so marvelous about this gift. It applies to us all, but it's also for each one. God died for *you*. He died for *me*. When you ask His forgiveness, and accept Him as your personal Savior, your sins are forgiven. And forgotten. They are as far from us as the East is from the West."

"As far as the East is from the West? What do you mean?"

"It's one of my favorite concepts in the Bible. People say that it's difficult to forgive and forget. I think it's actually easier to forgive a person for a wrong than to forget it ever happened."

Peggy nodded. "I'll never forget what's happened to me."

"The wonderful thing is that once you ask God for forgiveness, not only does He forgive you, but He *forgets*. God doesn't remember those sins from which you've repented, Peggy. The East is as far from the West as anything possibly can be. They both stretch into infinity. That's exactly how far God's mind is from your sins once you've repented of them. He doesn't keep them on file to look up again and be reminded of them. God has chosen not to remember your sin, Peggy. Christ died. His blood covered all those sins and now they're forgotten."

"As far as the East is from the West?"

"Exactly. Can you accept that, Peggy?"

"I can. I really can!" Impulsively, Peggy threw her arms around Mrs. Leighton's neck. "Now I know where she gets it."

Mrs. Leighton drew back and put her hands on Peggy's shoulders. "And what do you mean by that?"

"Lexi's faith. It comes from you, doesn't it?"

Mrs. Leighton smiled. "It comes from God, Peggy, and He offers it to you just like He offers it to us. It's what's going to get you through the next few weeks and months. You did the right thing by breaking up with Chad. You also did the right thing for your baby. Now you have to go forward. Get on with your life.

Lexi and I will help you in any way we can."

The three of them spent a short time in prayer right there in Lexi's bedroom, and when they were through, Peggy knew that her heart was clean and that God had truly forgiven her.

When Peggy left the Leightons' home later that afternoon, there was a bright, relaxed smile on her face. "Thank you, Lexi." Peggy gave her friend a hug. "Thank your mother again, too."

Peggy knew at last that she didn't have to go through the rest of her life alone. Her parents and the Lord would be at her side to guide her.

———

The day finally came. After weeks of work and anticipation, "Save Cedar River Day" was about to begin. Todd, Lexi and Peggy stood in the middle of the park amazed at the number of booths, displays and people.

Peggy was looking better and stronger each day. The conversation and prayer she'd had with Lexi's mother had set her on a new and different path. She'd not only accepted God's forgiveness, but had finally forgiven herself. When Chad saw how determined Peggy was, he left her alone and made no further attempts to threaten her. Lexi was grateful for that, although she had a hunch that Peggy's problems with Chad weren't over yet.

The band in the gazebo broke into song. In front of it, two hundred trees stood waiting to be planted. They had each been donated by concerned citizens of the community. Volunteers would plant the trees after an informative speech about how trees help the environment.

At the far end of the park, the ice cream social was just getting underway, with Binky and Jennifer's help. Egg and Ben were handing out copies of their newsletter.

Cedar River was looking wonderful. There were new trees along the riverbank and freshly painted boats sailed in the water. The trash and debris had vanished. There wasn't a scrap of paper, a straw or twig anywhere. Everyone was careful to use the trash bins placed throughout the park. For the first time in many days, Lexi's heart was light as a feather.

"I'm starved," Peggy announced. "Anyone for an ice cream cone? Todd's buying," she said teasingly.

"I am? Who says?"

"You're the one who's so good about saving your money," Peggy said pointedly. "So you're the logical one to treat us."

As they ate their cones, Lexi watched as Egg chased after a little boy who had dropped a scrap of paper on the ground. Patiently Egg instructed the child to pick it up and put it in the garbage bin. Lexi smiled happily as she gazed around the beautiful park. Being a steward of God's earth was much more fun than she ever dreamed it could be.

———

There's excitement and mystery in Cedar River! A famous star has come to town to play in a much publicized tennis tournament. When she is kidnapped, Todd, Lexi and the gang try to discover her whereabouts. Read about it in Cedar River Daydreams #12, *Vanishing Star*.

A Note From Judy

I'm glad you're reading *Cedar River Daydreams*! I hope I've given you something to think about as well as a story to entertain you. If you feel you have any of the problems that Lexi and her friends experience, I encourage you to talk with your parents, a pastor, or a trusted adult friend. There are many people who care about you!

Also, I enjoy hearing from my readers, so if you'd like to write, my address is:

Judy Baer
Bethany House Publishers
6820 Auto Club Road
Minneapolis, MN 55438

Please include an <u>addressed, stamped envelope</u> if you would like an answer. Thanks.